Angie, white-faced, trembled with anger. "It's true what Ellen said about my roommates, isn't it? 'Angie's out; she's in.' "

"Look, Angie, someone had to replace you. What did you expect?" Edie asked.

"A little . . . a little decency. The body's hardly cold. You don't even like Ellen—'gushing like her father's oil wells'—isn't that how you put it?"

"All right," Edie said. "So money matters to me. It matters to everyone who hasn't got it. You'll find out—now that you haven't got any. Wake up, Angie. It's a buy and sell world. I took you through Latin; you took me through the country club. That's what it's all about."

Angie shook her head. This was her *best friend* Edie talking! Suddenly her anger was gone, replaced by a hollow void. "I thought it was all about something else," she said softly, more to herself than to Edie. "I thought it was all about loyal friends."

Bestsellers from SIGNET VISTA

(0451)

- ☐ **THE BEST THAT MONEY CAN BUY by Anne Snyder and Louis Pelletier.** (125258—$2.25)*
- ☐ **NOBODY'S BROTHER by Anne Synder and Louis Pelletier.** (117565—$2.25)
- ☐ **TWO POINT ZERO by Anne Snyder and Louis Pelletier.** (114760—$1.75)*
- ☐ **GOODBYE, PAPER DOLL by Anne Snyder.** (124332—$2.25)
- ☐ **COUNTER PLAY by Anne Snyder.** (118987—$2.25)*
- ☐ **FIRST STEP by Anne Snyder.** (117573—$1.75)*
- ☐ **MY NAME IS DAVY—I'M AN ALCOHOLIC by Anne Snyder.** (123360—$1.95)*
- ☐ **TWO BLOCKS DOWN by Jina Delton.** (114779—$1.50)*
- ☐ **THE CLIFFS OF CAIRO by Elsa Marston.** (115309—$1.75)*
- ☐ **OVER THE HILL AT FOURTEEN by Jamie Callan.** (115740—$1.75)*
- ☐ **PLEASE DON'T KISS ME NOW by Merrill Joan Gerber.** (115759—$1.95)*
- ☐ **ANDREA by Jo Stewart.** (116542—$1.75)*
- ☐ **ALICE WITH GOLDEN HAIR by Eleanor Hull.** (117956—$1.95)*
- ☐ **A SHADOW LIKE A LEOPARD by Myron Levoy.** (117964—$2.25)*

*Prices slightly higher in Canada

Buy them at your local bookstore or use this convenient coupon for ordering.

THE NEW AMERICAN LIBRARY, INC.,
P.O. Box 999, Bergenfield, New Jersey 07621

Please send me the books I have checked above. I am enclosing $_____
(please add $1.00 to this order to cover postage and handling). Send check or money order—no cash or C.O.D.'s. Prices and numbers are subject to change without notice.

Name_____

Address_____

City _____ State _____ Zip Code _____
Allow 4-6 weeks for delivery.
This offer is subject to withdrawal without notice.

THE BEST THAT MONEY CAN BUY

by
Anne Snyder and Louis Pelletier

A SIGNET VISTA BOOK
NEW AMERICAN LIBRARY
TIMES MIRROR

PUBLISHER'S NOTE

This novel is a work of fiction. Names, characters, places, and incidents are either the product of the author's imagination or are used fictitiously, and any resemblance to actual persons, living or dead, events, or locales is entirely coincidental.

NAL BOOKS ARE AVAILABLE AT QUANTITY DISCOUNTS WHEN USED TO PROMOTE PRODUCTS OR SERVICES. FOR INFORMATION PLEASE WRITE TO PREMIUM MARKETING DIVISION, THE NEW AMERICAN LIBRARY, INC., 1633 BROADWAY, NEW YORK, NEW YORK 10019.

RL4/IL6+

SIGNET VISTA TRADEMARK REG. U.S. PAT. OFF. AND FOREIGN COUNTRIES
REGISTERED TRADEMARK—MARCA REGISTRADA
HECHO EN CHICAGO, U.S.A.

SIGNET, SIGNET CLASSIC, MENTOR, PLUME, MERIDIAN and NAL BOOKS are published by The New American Library, Inc., 1633 Broadway, New York, New York 10019

First Printing, October, 1983

1 2 3 4 5 6 7 8 9

PRINTED IN THE UNITED STATES OF AMERICA

This book is dedicated, with heartfelt thanks and love, to my friend, my teacher, Sylvain Bernstein, for his devotion over many years to me and countless other writers.

Anne Snyder

Chapter One

The call from her mother came on the day before spring vacation. With a numb, helpless feeling Angie hung up the phone. At first, disbelief. It couldn't be. Then a moment of self-pity. It was true. Then anger. Why? Why couldn't she come back to Oakmont for next semester?

"Darling," her mother had said. "I can't go into it over the phone. "I'll tell you when you get home."

"But, Mom . . ."

"Bring home your clothes, and your typewriter, and your guitar. And Angie, don't forget the riding boots you loaned to Edie."

"Why? I don't . . ."

"Angie, just come home. I can't talk about it now." And it had sounded as if her mother was crying or grabbing for a tissue or something because the phone squawked, grated, went dead. And that was it.

Angie put down the phone and took deep breaths. She tried to remember her mantra from last year when they were all into Zen, but the magic words weren't there. She looked at her watch. Biology at eleven. With practiced reflex, she picked up her notebook, held it a moment, dropped it listlessly on the desk.

Then a stab of anxiety. What if something were wrong

with Daddy? No, scratch that. Not thinkable. Nothing was ever wrong with Daddy. Then what?

The bell rang for the five-minute break between classes. Angie looked out the window of her room at the small quadrangle, the court, they called it, enclosed by the four redwood and glass buildings that made up Oakmont. "Girls ten to eighteen, college preparation," the brochure had said. "Riding, field trips, sailing. Senior semester in France."

Angie watched the girls crossing the court to change classes. Gloria turned and waved, motioned for her to hurry along to biology. But Angie stood there. She could see the distant ocean flashing sunlight on the red tiled roofs of Santa Barbara. No, she couldn't be leaving this. There was some mistake. Her father would take care of it. Of course he would.

She waited till the court was empty, then turned from the window.

She left the room by the back stairs and took the winding path that led down the hill toward the stables. She gave her favorite chestnut mare a pat on the nose and a lump of sugar. Then she sat on the corral fence and felt like a total, hopeless idiot as the splat of a tear hit her hand. Ridiculous. Sentimental. Absurd. "Dear Abby . . . I am a sixteen year old student, my mother just phoned me . . ."

The chestnut mare nudged her for another lump of sugar. Angie kissed her on the nose, gave her the sugar. All of a sudden, she knew what she would do. Call her father. How simple. How perfect. He'd clear it all up in two seconds, just as he always did.

She ran all the way back to her room, grabbed the phone, a lifeline, and dialed the operator.

"Collect call, please, Los Angeles, person-to-person, Mr. James Careau, at 213-077-2724."

"Thank you," said the operator.

There was a long wait. "I'm sorry," the operator said. "That number has been disconnected."

"No, no, there's some mistake," Angie said. "That's a large business office, Careau Investments—on Wilshire Boulevard." Angie repeated the number.

"I'll try again," said the operator.

The wait was not so long this time.

"I'm sorry; that number has been disconnected."

"Thank you," Angie said, barely audible.

She took her suitcases out of the closet and began throwing things into them in jerky, panicky motions.

The clock ticked loudly. She couldn't sleep. Why not put on the light, wake both of them, and tell them? They'd understand. She listened to their breathing. Gloria, light, ladylike; Edie, deep and serious. Her roommates, her friends. Not just friends. There was a special closeness between them, a sharing: clothes, boys, troubles, dreams. Two years. Inseparable. But tell them what?

" 'Ay, there's the rub,' " she said to herself. Shakespeare II, Miss Emory, seminar for juniors only.

She looked at the illuminated clock. 4 A.M. Miserable night thoughts crowded in on her. Images. Miss Emory looking over her glasses. "The next line, Angela." Angela mouthed silently. " 'Ay, there's the rub. For in that sleep of death what dreams may come?' "

Wow, come off it, girl. Think of something cheerful. Ryan. Think of darling Ryan. Adorable Ryan. So what's Ryan going to say when he finds out? Finds out what?

She rolled over and stared into the blackness of the ceiling. Okay, one day he finds out you're not the beauty he thinks. And you're too skinny. A hundred and nine pounds and your hair isn't even blond; it's mouse. A California girl with mouse hair.

She had an urge to run into the bathroom and look at herself in the mirror. What she had to remember was the other day in the pool when Edie had said, "I wish I had your shape, Angie." So she did have an acceptable figure, and she supposed her face would get by. The mouse hair, turned under in a smooth pageboy, gave her a kind of pixie look, and she was often told that her husky voice was sort of sexy and surprising for a girl as slight as she was. Okay, so she was a five-and-a-half in the looks department; maybe she was a six. Gloria was a positive ten. And Edie? Well, Edie got straight A's, so her face didn't really matter.

What if? What if? Why was Daddy's number disconnected? He'd explain, of course, and then it would be all right. But what if it were some dreaded disease or something awful like that? Cancer. Or a divorce. Half the girls in the school had stepparents.

Om, mani, padme hum. Ah, there was that mantra she had been trying to remember. That would put her to sleep. She began to say the words softly to herself.

"Angie?" It was Edie.

"Huh?"

"You okay?"

"Sure."

A pause, then: "Want something to eat?"

"No, thanks."

"You got anything to eat?"

Angie smiled in the dark. "Sorry."

"Okay. 'Night."

" 'Night."

What was she going to tell them when they saw she was taking all her things home? She took a deep breath. *"Om, mani, padme hum."*

The alarm rang at seven-thirty.

It was easier than she thought. She just told them she was bringing stuff home to be cleaned. And since she usually took her guitar and saddle, she only had to explain the typewriter. And since no one listened to what anyone was saying in the dizzy excitement of the first day of the spring break, the typewriter, saddle, and suitcases came downstairs without comment, and the moment of departure seemed minutes after they woke up.

Gloria had a red Rabbit convertible, the most envied car on the campus. Gloria was the most envied girl, even though she was only a junior. Gloria looked as if she had been born on the beach at Malibu; she almost had been but her mother had made it to the hospital at Santa Monica just in time. Gloria knew, of course, that she was a little more than attractive, but the nice thing was that she had next to zero in self confidence; she spilled things on her best clothes, had trouble reciting in class, and looked on Edie as her role model. Of course, she did get an A in modern dance.

Edie was one of three students on scholarship. Offering Oakmont scholarships looked good on the brochure and helped extract contributions from alumni, but even realizing all that, Edie was a happy recipient. Her father taught high school and her mother, a gentle alcoholic, painted unsalable abstractions.

The red Rabbit, with top open to the sun, pulled away from the dorm building. Scrunched down with all her gear, Angie sat in the rear seat.

She didn't want to look back as they passed through the big iron gates. Even knowing she wouldn't be back, she didn't want to say good-bye to anybody.

But Edie looked back, raised her arm in mock salute. "Hail and farewell." She grinned at Angie.

"Oh, shut up, Edie," Angie said and dug herself deeper into the back seat.

Edie turned around. "What's the matter with her?"

Gloria laughed. "Maybe she can't bear to leave dear old Oakmont."

Edie shook her head. "Vacation neurosis, that's what it is. And we haven't even gotten to the bottom of the hill."

Gloria took the coast highway south. She drove briskly, only slightly aware of the incredible beauty of the ocean crashing in brilliant bursts of white against the cliffs below.

The wind clutched at the little red convertible, twisting Gloria's hair into wild tangles. Edie grabbed the hair and tied it back, yelling some crazy Oscar Wilde poem about "bright golden hair."

The day was irresistible, soaked with sudden freedom, lifted above the dead weight of books and term papers and French subjunctives; ahead, the limitless possibilities of spring vacation. Who could resist?

Angie could. But not for long. She had to sit up, and the fabulous day grabbed hold of her and carried her along, getting inside her head and saying maybe she was making too much of her mother's call. Maybe it was one of those wild surprises that Daddy came up with, like the trip to Europe last summer. Maybe they were going someplace. Hey, maybe he was retiring in glory at age forty-five, and they were all going off to live in Tahiti. She laughed out loud, and Edie turned around and gave her a thumbs-up signal and yelled to Gloria, "Look who's come back from the dead!"

They always brought along sandwiches and Cokes and always stopped at a huge rock that looked down on the ocean. And they talked vacation talk. Parties, shows, shopping.

Boys.

"Eddie Stearns," Gloria said.

"No," Edie said. "He clutches."

Gloria had a large roster of boys, and she was setting Edie up with one of her spares.

"Dave what's-his-name. The surfer."

Edie shook her head. "Uh-uh."

"Why not? He has a cute little MG."

"He also has an overactive libido."

Gloria grinned. "That's bad?"

"You get a ride in the cute little MG and he expects the ultimate sacrifice."

Angie couldn't help laughing. "What if he had a Porsche?"

"I'd think it over." Edie smiled and bit into her sandwich.

Wonderful freedom, limitless possibilities. The usual big party at Gloria's house, the tickets for the ballet, the beach parties.

"What are you doing with Ryan?" Gloria asked Angie.

"A leading question," Edie mumbled over her sandwich.

Gloria laughed. "Cut it out, Edie."

Edie smiled with a lump of sandwich in her cheek. She touched Angie's arm affectionately. "She knows I'm kidding. If I had someone as beautiful as Ryan . . ." She looked up into the sky, leaving the sentence hanging.

Angie laughed again, seeing Ryan, projecting him onto the screen in her head, seeing him coming up the driveway, jumping out of his car, running to her. The kiss, the wonderful closeness as he held her.

Gloria drained the last of her Coke, looked at Edie. "How about Bob?"

"He's yours."

"Was."

"What happened?" Edie included Angie in the question. "Why weren't we informed?" She gave Gloria a mock look of woe. "Not the ultimate sacrifice?"

Gloria shook her head. "He scares me. He talks about computers. He has a plan for robbing banks without even leaving his house."

"My kinda guy," Edie said. "Give him my phone number."

They laughed because everything was just a bit ridiculous on the first day of vacation. And they finished the sandwiches and looked at a boy and girl in swimsuits, holding hands, walking along the beach.

"Touching," Edie said with an exaggerated sigh.

"I wonder what he's saying to her?" Angie said.

"The usual," Gloria answered.

"No," Edie said, "not yet. They're just getting acquainted. He's considering the angles."

"But her father has warned her against his type," Gloria added.

"Ah, but she loves to play with fire," Edie said.

Angie laughed. What a wonderful pair of friends she had. Then it hit her. She was going to lose them. She wasn't going back to school. She stopped laughing. "Let's go," she said abruptly. "My mother's expecting me."

Edie turned in her seat. "Hey, what happened?"

Gloria looked in the rearview mirror. "Adolescent mood swings. She needs a little therapy."

"I just need to get home if it's okay with you."

"Yeah, sure," Gloria said. "At your service, princess." She turned the key in the ignition.

Angie dug into the seat and looked resolutely up into the sky. She disliked herself for talking that way to Gloria. What she should do was come right out and tell them everything.

What was everything?

Gloria pulled out onto the highway, and the sudden blast of a horn made her yank the wheel and jam on the brakes. A car swooshed by inches away, the driver yelling loud curses. The Rabbit stalled, and Gloria sat there trembling at the brush with disaster.

Angie wanted to say it was her fault, but she couldn't. Gloria had been distracted by Angie's sudden, harsh words.

Gloria started the engine and cautiously edged the Rabbit into the right lane.

They drove in silence. Angie tried to think of something funny, something to put the first day of vacation back on track, but the words wouldn't come. She felt guilty for spoiling the mood, the mindless fun. She felt, suddenly, unaccountably guilty for everything in the world.

Edie turned the radio on to a rock station, and they listened inattentively. They passed Cabrillo Beach, watching the surfers in black wet suits, sitting on their boards like performing seals waiting for a ringmaster's cue.

At a stoplight above Malibu, a souped-up pickup filled wih surfers pulled alongside. Whistles of appreciation directed at the girls in the Rabbit pulled Angie up from her seat.

The light changed and the pickup roared ahead with thumbs-up signals of approval. Edie lifted her thumb in reply. The vacation was back on track.

Edie lived way down in Venice, a wild, improbable enclave on the ocean near Santa Monica. Venice was filled with types, non-standard individualists who seemed unaware of their eccentricities, who did their own thing long after such things were not done anymore.

Edie's mother and father lived there because they had found a place in the cheaper section, but subtly, unspoken between Edie and her father, also because it was easier to manage Edie's mother there. She could shuffle out to the beach in her slippers and bathrobe, set up her easel, smear meaningless daubs of paint on canvas, and no one would notice, except those who stopped occasionally and nodded their heads and said something like, "What deep emotional value!" Edie's mother, who floated euphorically in her alcoholic fog, was always pleased. She had dozens of friends in the neighborhood and was considered a real personality.

Edie's father taught high school math and had gone to college with one of the trustees of Oakmont. It was through this connection that he had wangled Edie's scholarship.

Edie made no apologies for her parents or the place where she lived. Gloria and Angie loved to sleep over in the cramped little apartment only a half block from the beach. Edie's mother was amusing when sober and gentle and loving after her third vodka of the morning. Edie loved her fiercely and protected her against a disapproving world.

The Rabbit turned off the highway and up the hill to Sunset Boulevard. Edie was staying the weekend with Gloria, so they would take Angie to Bel-Air first.

Soon they turned off Sunset and drove through the impressive gates of Bel-Air. Angie sat up, her heart pounding, as the Rabbit mounted the curving road with the high hedges that concealed the limitless wealth of the houses behind them.

Angie's house was set discreetly back from the road, sited low into a lushly flowered hillside that looked down on the pool and tennis court. A curving driveway led to the broad slate entrance terrace. Behind it were high glass windows that went the length of the house. In the center was the huge oak doorway and, hidden to the right, the four-car garage.

They unloaded Angie's stuff and made dozens of wild arrangements to meet, which ended up with, "Okay, I'll call you."

Angie watched the Rabbit leave the driveway and disappear behind the roadside hedges. She looked through the glass of the living room, expecting to see her mother or Norma, the maid, or somebody, but nothing moved in the house.

She touched the front door button and heard the chimes ring uselessly back in the kitchen. She hit the button several more times, then began rummaging through her purse for the key, which she knew she didn't have.

Without even thinking about it, she walked toward the garage. Back in the old days, long before they moved to Bel-Air and lived in a modest house in the San Fernando Valley, they always kept a key in an empty box of rat poison in the garage. The habit stuck; in Bel-Air, rats were taken care of by a man who arrived and departed unseen at regular intervals. Angie found the key in the toe of an old ski boot.

She opened the front door of the house and put her suitcases and guitar and typewriter inside. "Hey, I'm home!" she yelled, more as an act of bravado in case any strangers might be lurking than to announce her arrival. Then she yelled again, "Hey, Duke!"

Duke was a mutt without positive ancestry. He was mostly black, medium-sized, and of indefinite age. He was white around the muzzle and was probably pretty old. He was Angie's dog, found in the park years ago and named after Duke Hooper, a rock star, who was Angie's idol at the time.

Duke, in the tradition of lousy watchdogs, slept through anything and loved everyone. He came down the hall from the bedrooms and ran stiff-legged to Angie, whining an ecstatic greeting.

She hugged Duke, wondering where everyone was, then went back to the kitchen. It was strange about Norma. This wasn't her day off.

"Where's Norma, Duke? Where's Mom?" Duke pointed to the refrigerator and did a little dance of expectancy. Angie opened the refrigerator door. There wasn't much; some cold cuts, a wilted salad, three bottles of diet cola, and one half bottle of wine. She wondered if a sip of the wine would make this awful empty, slightly scary feeling go away. Maybe it would. Or maybe a diet cola. Or how about half cola, half wine?

She threw Duke a piece of ham, took out a bottle of cola, rejected the wine, and sat down at the kitchen table. She pulled the tab on the cola and felt absolutely awful, as if she were sitting on the edge of a high place that was going to collapse and drop her into a terrifying nowhere.

She sipped the cola and glanced out at the swimming

pool. Everything seemed deserted. The key to the house lay on the kitchen table before her. She stared at it, remembering it was always a rule that you put the key back in place as soon as you opened the door. That had been the rule way back when they used to live in the Valley. . . .

Chapter Two

It was back in the Valley, when she was twelve going on thirteen, that she had found the black mutt and named him Duke. He had been scrounging dejectedly in a garbage container and ran away when he saw her. She would have let him go, except that he stood under a bush and wagged his tail hopefully, and she had half a gooey cupcake left over from school lunch. So she put it on the grass and told him to come get it. He ran out from under the bush, grabbed the cupcake, and disappeared.

She walked home unhurriedly, enjoying the spring day, thinking casually about the dog. There were others like him in the quiet, tree-shaded neighborhood. They were scroungers who lived off the involuntary bounty of the middle-income householders whose middle-income garbage cans, while not so luxurious as a scrounger could find in Beverly Hills, were, nonetheless, adequate.

Angie lived in a three-and-a-den at the end of a dead-end street. It was white stucco and had a flaming red bougainvillea over the doorway. There was a small yard in back with a barbecue. And there was a basketball hoop over the garage door for her brother, Nick, who was fifteen, stuck-up, girl crazy, and a terrible pain in the neck.

When Angie got home, the mutt was already there

ahead of her in the driveway, dancing lightly, ready to run, but wagging his tail hopefully.

Angie sat on the front doorstep. She smiled and said, "Hi, Duke," that being her favorite name at the time. The mutt ran to her and smothered her with such pent-up, unused love that she was overwhelmed.

When Nick came home from basketball practice and passed her room, he said, "What's that awful smell?"

"What awful smell?" she answered.

"That awful smell in your room."

"What awful smell in my room?"

Conversation between Angie and Nick tended to be one-dimensional. They were centuries apart, he in high school, she still in junior high.

Nick looked in the doorway. "Where did you get that awful mutt?"

Duke wagged his tail and did his dance, with no takers.

"He's not an awful mutt. He's a Labrador."

"He stinks."

"I'm going to wash him." ·

"You can't keep him."

"Who says?"

"Mom says."

"How do you know?"

"I know."

"Oh, do you now?"

Nick looked at Angie witheringly. He really didn't know at first what his mother would say about the dog. But what he did know—for certain—was that, somehow, Angie would get to keep the mutt. What really infuriated him was that, with no demands, no arguments, Angie could always win her parents over . . . particularly her father. What was worse, she did it innocently, unaware that she was doing it. And Nick—with a jealous passion—hated her for it. And he resented his parents for stupidly falling for her sickeningly sweet ways. It wasn't fair; he always fought for whatever privileges he got.

He stared at her until she looked away. "Angie, you disgust me, you actually do."

"I actually disgust you."

"Yes, you actually do. You have the mind of a midget."

"Some midgets are very bright," Angie said cuttingly.

Nick looked at his sister with revulsion, picked up a book from her desk, and flipped it at Duke. The mutt dodged and scrambled under the bed. Nick sauntered down the hall to his room.

Angie ran out into the hall. "You . . . you troglodyte!" she yelled furiously. She had just learned the word in a class on prehistoric man and had immediately forgotten what it meant, but it had a good rolling sound to it, kind of like a witch's curse or a high-class version of "drop dead."

She coaxed Duke out from under the bed, gave him some scraps from the refrigerator, and put him in her bathtub. The poor mutt had never had a bath and looked up at her with pitiful pleas for mercy. But when she dried him and let him loose in the yard, he ran wildly around and around like a pup. Then he jumped into her lap and covered her with kisses. Angie vowed on the spot that she would leave home if her mother wouldn't let her keep him.

The rest of the afternoon she tried to give the mutt a quick course in good manners. He really wanted to please. He learned "sit" in no time, and he fetched a tennis ball as if he had always played with children in families where tennis balls were available.

Angie heard her mother's car come into the driveway as the electric door opened. The door was a recent extravagance that her mother said they really didn't need, even if everyone on the block did have one. But it was, she did admit, a convenience.

Angie visualized her mother's moves: the groceries out

of the back of the lumpy station wagon, the deposit of milk and cheese in the refrigerator, the canned stuff on the shelves. Her mother would have on jeans and a casual sweater and be quite unaware of how smashing she looked. Angie thought her mother was probably one of the most beautiful women she had ever seen—gray eyes, black shining hair, a complexion that never needed even a touch of makeup—and, unlike some of her classmates, Angie never cringed when her mother called for her at school.

Angie knew, of course, that her mother had some basic flaws of character. For one thing, she could be awfully square, hanging around when Angie had some boys and girls over for a party, or not letting her ride in a car with Randy Hopper just because some people said he drank—which he did. He totaled his car on the very day Angie and a friend would have been with him if her mother hadn't said no. But it was the principle of the thing. Angie wouldn't have gone with Randy on a bet, but she hated to be told she couldn't.

Of course, she could understand about her mother, kind of. She had visited back in Regina, Iowa, one summer and stayed with Grandma and Grandpa Turner in the very house where Mom had been born. Grandma and Grandpa were really into religion. Sundays were a total disaster; other than going to church, not a single thing was allowed. Mom didn't seem to mind; she was right at home in Squaresville. But the summer wasn't a total washout. Angie, age eleven, had fallen in love with a horse at the village stables and had spent endless hours with him.

Angie often wondered how a dashing extrovert like her father ever got together with her mother. They were night and day, the lion and the lamb. No, not the lamb; Mom could be tough. She could say no, and you could point out that all the other kids were doing it, whatever it was, and Mom could put the other kids in their places and look you right in the eye and say no and mean it. Like the Randy Hopper thing.

"Angie . . . ?"

Well, here we go, Angie said to herself. She came in the kitchen and gave her mother a good hug.

"Hi, Mom. Listen, don't say no till I tell you the complete circumstances."

Mom was looking through the screen door into the yard. "Where did that dog come from?"

"Well . . . that's the circumstances."

Mom tapped on the screen. "Scat! Shoo! Go home!"

Duke stood wagging his tail, doing his dance of obeisance.

"Mom, this is his home. I want to keep him."

"Angie, how many times have I told you . . ."

"Mom, he can sit. I taught him this afternoon. Duke, sit!"

Duke stood and wagged his tail, hopefully.

"Angie . . ."

It was a desperate ploy but Angie had to try it. "Mom, Nick says I can't keep him."

"Nick says?"

"Yeah, he said Duke stank but I washed him. Can Nick tell me I can't keep him?" She took her mother's hand, held it tightly. "Can Duke stay till Daddy comes home and we can have a discussion with the pros and cons and all? Can we, Mom?"

Mom, whose name was Kathy, smiled. "Angie, you're a better con artist than your father."

"Oh, Mom! Thank you!"

"I didn't say yes."

"But, we'll see?" Angie asked eagerly.

"Okay," Kathy said, "we'll see."

"When Daddy comes home" had been iffy this past year. Angie didn't quite know what Daddy did—something about investments, whatever they were—but Daddy had his own business and stayed late almost every night, and some nights he'd call and say he was taking a client out to dinner. Nick new more about Daddy's business and said Daddy was making a pile, and he was going to hit Daddy for a car of his own on his sixteenth birthday.

Daddy missed dinner and got home at nine. He went right to Angie's room where she was doing her homework, gave her a tremendous bear hug, and handed her the book she'd been wanting with all the horse pictures in it.

Daddy had "landed a big one," she learned in the kitchen, where he was sitting with Mom and having a glass of beer. The "big one" was a new client who had a frightening amount of money to invest, and Daddy was going to invest it for him. And then Daddy whipped out a fancy brochure with pictures of a BMW sports coupe, and Mom saw the piece written in the salesman's handwriting and said, "We can't afford it." And Daddy laughed and said that at least we could afford another bottle of beer.

Angie knew it was the perfect moment for introducing the dog.

But Daddy was ahead of her. "Whose cute little mutt is that peeking through the back fence?"

And before Mom could cut in, Angie said, "He's yours, Daddy," and told the story of the discovery of Duke.

Daddy listened with a smile, saw that Mom wasn't going to let Duke live in the house, and solved the whole thing by saying Duke could stay in the yard, and they'd build him a doghouse. Be good to have a watchdog, anyway.

Angie had known Daddy would solve it. He always did. Daddy made things happen. It was easy for him. She didn't know that sometimes it was a little too easy.

"Happy birthday," Nick said without looking up from the sports page propped in front of the breakfast cereal box.

"Thanks," Angie answered. "But you didn't have to say it."

"Sure, I had to say it. Mom said I had to say it." He mimicked Kathy: " 'Don't forget to say happy birthday to your sister.' " He looked up from the paper. "How old are you, anyway?"

"Thirteen," Angie said with great dignity.

He shook his head sadly.

"What's so terrible about that?"

"Thirteen," he said scornfully.

"You were thirteen two years ago. I gave you a book."

"Yeah, that's right, a book."

"Well, at least I gave you something."

"I'm giving you something," he said. "Mom bought it."

Angie sat up eagerly. "What is it, Nick?"

"How do I know? She bought it."

Nick shoved his plate away, stood up, picked his book bag off the kitchen counter, and walked out the back door. Why should he stick around and watch the enormous fuss made over Angie's birthday? He knew Dad had gone overboard to surprise Angie with a gift she hadn't even asked for.

He remembered his own thirteenth birthday. He'd wanted a moped so badly, he'd begged and cajoled for weeks; even threatened to leave home if he didn't get one. But Mom had said they couldn't afford it, and he was too young, and a moped was dangerous. And good old Dad had gone along with her. What he'd gotten, instead, were binoculars. Binoculars! He'd shoved them in his drawer under his T-shirts, and they were still there.

As he crossed the yard, Duke came rushing up to greet him, but Nick ignored the proffered greeting.

When Mom came in the kitchen, she gave Angie a terrific birthday hug, and then Daddy whirled her around, and it started to be a real birthday, with a half-dozen presents and squeals of delight from Angie. But the kicker was the present from Daddy. It was a plain white envelope with birthday greetings on the front. And as she opened it, she couldn't help but notice her mother's slightly disapproving look in contrast to Daddy's grin of anticipation.

Angie was speechless. She looked up at her father and burst into tears.

He laughed and took her in his arms. "You don't like it, huh?"

Angie blubbered some more, clutched the envelope, and said thank you, thank you, thank you, so many times that they were all relieved when a horn sounded for Angie's car pool outside. Holding onto the envelope, she kissed them both and said so many more thank you's they had to shove her out the door to get her to school. Then she rushed back in to get the books she'd forgotten in her room. In all the excitement, she couldn't remember where she had put them. She stood in her doorway, trying to think. Then she heard her parents' voices:

"She seemed to like your present," Mom said.

"Yeah, she seemed to."

"Jim, I really think . . ."

"Hey, honey," Dad interrupted, "we've been over this. It's done. Angie's happy, I'm happy. So come on in. Be happy."

"I really think that twenty dollars a half hour for riding lessons for a thirteen year old . . ."

"Kathy," he said firmly. "It's done."

Angie's eyes scanned the room, but the voices from the kitchen again caught her attention:

"I suppose you put it on the credit card," Mom's voice said.

"Of course I put it on the credit card."

"Oh, Jim . . ."

"Now look, baby . . ."

"Jim, twenty dollars a half hour for riding lessons . . ."

"It's the best riding school in the valley. And anyway, it isn't riding. It's called junior equitation."

Angie stood there uncomfortably, not wanting to eavesdrop, but still unable to move.

"I suppose she'll need boots," her mother said. "And the next thing you know . . ."

"I've already bought the boots," Dad said. "I probably got the wrong size."

"Which credit card?"

"Master Charge."

"We already owe them twenty-five hundred from last month."

Angie heard her father laugh. "Good," he said, "they need the business."

"Jim, really . . ."

"Kathy, Kathy, come off it. We're on our way up. The more you owe, the richer you are. It's the new economics."

There was a still moment, then Mom said, "Will you be home for dinner?"

"Iffy. I'll call you."

"You don't have to. I'll keep something warm just in case."

Angie heard the scrape of a chair along with Dad's voice. "Happy birthday to you too, Kathy. You gave us a great kid."

Another silence, then: "Hey, do you remember . . ." he said.

Mom laughed. "That awful ride to the hospital."

Dad joined her laughter. "Thirteen years. Where'd they go?"

"Good years," Mom answered.

"Getting better, believe me," Dad said.

"But fifteen riding lessons at twenty dollars. Three hundred dollars." Mom paused. "Well, I guess it's not the end of the world."

Angie's car pool horn blasted insistently. She located her books at the foot of her bed, grabbed them up, and ran out.

She'd had a good birthday—that thirteenth one—but somehow it had felt just a bit tarnished at the edges.

The black mood, the scary, uneasy feeling didn't go away. Angie had willed herself back to the Valley, back to twelve years old, going on thirteen, but it didn't help. She was here and now in Bel-Air, sixteen going on seventeen, sitting in the kitchen wondering what had happened. Or if anything had happened.

Oh, something had happened, all right. She wasn't going back to school. That was for sure. And Daddy's business? She reached back to the counter and pulled up the phone, dialed hastily. Again, that voice. It sounded like the same one she had heard in Santa Barbara. "I'm sorry," said the voice, "that number has been disconnected."

Angie jumped up with a feeling of panic. She suddenly felt she had to get outside, into the open air, as if that would free her of the weight of the empty house. She opened the kitchen door and went down toward the pool. And there, hidden from sight on the far side, was Nick, lolling on a chaise with a drink in his hand. He looked at her disinterestedly, raised his glass in mock salute.

"Nick! I didn't know you were here. Didn't you hear me yell when I came in?"

"Yeah, I heard you."

"Well, at least you could have said hello or hi or something."

"Hi or something," he said in a flat voice.

Exasperating. Frustrating. She could never talk to him. Those miles apart had never gotten any closer over the years. He went his own way, never getting closer to any of them, Dad, Mother, herself; he lived a veiled, separate, closed-out life. He was a sophomore now, at USC. He had his own car, a Mercedes roadster, his own friends—all very rich—his own life-style.

Angie sat on a chair, drew a deep breath. "Nick, what's happening?"

"I'm having a mild Scotch on the rocks, sipping slowly, enjoying it, and after I've finished, I'm going into the pool. That's what's happening."

"Oh, Nick . . ."

He looked at her indifferently. "I hear you got yanked out of Oakmont."

"Yes, yes, I did. Why, Nick? What's going on?"

"I'm not going back to USC." He noticed that her expression didn't change. What made her think that being taken out of that idiot girls' school was as important as his having to leave college? But there was nothing new about that, was there? She had always come first in this family, hadn't she?

She broke into his thoughts: "Why, Nick?" She was on the edge of tears. "What is it? Where's Daddy? Why isn't he here?"

"It's just possible that Daddy's down at the district attorney's office answering some embarrassing questions. Or maybe he's skipped town. Who knows?"

She looked at him in utter desolation. "Stop making fun of me."

"I kid you not, sister."

"And don't talk like some crummy TV character!"

Nick smiled. He loved to rile her; it was so easy. "You want a drink, Angie?"

"No."

"What's the matter, don't the precious little Oakmont princesses ever touch a drop? I'll bet they do. And more. I'll bet that high and mighty Gloria puts out on occasion, doesn't she?"

Angie clenched her fists. Once she had thrown a pitcher of milk at him, and the cut on his head had been awful.

She waited a long time, controlling her fury. Then she said softly, "Nick, please?"

He looked away, down at the pool. "He's in trouble, real trouble. But it's not in the open yet. I don't know the details. He's under investigation for something that has a fancy name and means he misused other people's money."

"He didn't," Angie said hotly.

He turned to her. "Didn't he?"

"Daddy isn't a cheat; he wouldn't misuse anything."

"Angie, have you got the faintest idea what your father does for a living?"

"Of course. He's an investment counselor; he owns his own business, Careau Investments."

"Gone."

"What do you mean, gone? He has an office on Wilshire Boulevard."

"Had an office. He couldn't pay the rent. They threw him out on the street."

"You're lying!"

"Okay, I'm lying. How about being a nice kid and going in and getting me the Scotch bottle?" He looked at her with sudden revulsion. "Oh, for pete's sake, don't start bawling."

Helpless tears were running down Angie's cheeks. "You're lying," she said. "It's one of your stories."

"Yeah, sure, I'm making it all up. You want to know the really crummy part? The really cheap, second-rate scenario? I'd invited Barbara Stender here to stay with us for the spring break. She'll be here Wednesday. You know who Barbara Stender is?"

Angie hid her face and her tears.

"Barbara Stender is only the daughter of Stender Data Processing. I mean, her old man practically owns Silicon Valley."

"When's Daddy coming home?" Angie asked in a low voice.

"So what if this gets in the papers when Barbara's here? What'll I look like?"

"When's Daddy coming home?"

"Who knows? He's probably out beating the bushes for enough coin to keep the mortgage boys off our backs. You know how much the payments are on this house?"

Angie got up and walked slowly to the living room doors and went into the house. She had left her bags standing in the hall. She went down to her room and sat in her rocking chair, the only piece left from her days in the Valley.

Duke came in, wagging his rear. She sat there rubbing Duke's ears and saying to herself, Nick is a liar; it couldn't be, it's just one of his stories. But she could hear the disembodied voice, the operator. "I'm sorry; that number has been disconnected."

Chapter Three

Around and around inside her head, the unanswered questions. Angie must have sat in the rocking chair in her room for hours. Then she heard the sound of her mother's car in the driveway.

She ran down the hall and flung open the front door. They were in each other's arms, hugging, she saying, "Mom, oh, Mom," over and over, and Kathy saying, "Baby, baby, are you all right?" as if Angie had just come home from some harrowing journey.

Angie helped Kathy bring groceries into the kitchen, and they chattered without direction, putting off the real questions. "How have you been? Let me look at you," from Kathy. "How are Gloria and Edie? Did you eat anything? Oh, Angie, are you getting thinner?"

Angie put away the groceries and turned to really look at her mother. She drew her breath in sharply. She hadn't been home since Christmas and the change in her mother was startling, like one of those actresses in a tour de force, aging imperceptibly from scene to scene.

Oh, not that her mother wasn't as attractive as ever, but there were noticeable deep frown lines now, and tight downward curves around her mouth, dark shadows under her eyes, and a nervous tapping of her fingers on the kitchen counter.

It must be bad, Angie thought, if it had done this to her mother.

Kathy was holding up the pot. "I'm having coffee."

"Me too," Angie said. She busied herself getting out the cream and wondering what they could have for a snack. The refrigerator again struck her as strangely empty, and some pieces of cheese were all she could find.

Kathy saw her searching the refrigerator. "We don't keep it quite so full now that Norma's gone. Did you know that Norma was gone?" Kathy asked, turning her back and fussing with the coffee pot.

"Did she go back to . . . where was it?"

"Fresno. No, I found another place for her."

Kathy poured the coffee. They sat at the table, Kathy drumming on the Formica top with her finger.

"Mom . . ."

"It's a mess, Angie, a terrible mess."

Angie waited, then said, "And I'm not going back to Oakmont?"

Kathy nodded. Then, irrelevantly, "Did you remember to bring home your saddle?"

"Yes."

Kathy warmed her hands around the coffee cup. "That was a terribly expensive saddle."

"Mom, what is this? What happened? Nick says that Daddy . . ."

"I don't know what happened!" The coffee sloshed over Kathy's hands; she dropped the cup into the saucer. "This young man came here one day about three weeks ago, very polite, nice looking young man. He said he was from the district attorney's office and he had an appointment with your father. They went into the library and talked a long time and finally the young man left." Kathy looked down into her cup. "Your father came out. I asked him. I said, 'Jim, what is it, what's the matter?' He just smiled and gave me that little girl hug, you know, the you-wouldn't-understand-don't-bother-your-pretty-head hug.''

"Where is Daddy?"

Kathy sighed heavily, looked at her watch. "Right now, he's arriving in Houston, Texas."

The look of despair on Angie's face gave Kathy a stab of pain.

"Texas?" Angie said slowly.

"He said he'd call us tonight."

"Mom . . ."

"Angie, Angie, I don't know! I don't know anything. He never tells me anything. I know he didn't pay your tuition; that's why you're not going back to school. I know the house payments are overdue. . . ."

Kathy's cup was rattling with the nervous movements of her hands. Angie got up and put her arms around her mother.

"Later, baby," Kathy said in a low voice. "We'll talk about it later, okay?"

"Okay, Mom."

Angie kissed the top of her mother's head and walked slowly out of the kitchen.

"Angie . . ."

"Yes, Mom?"

"Don't put the saddle in your room. Put it in the garage."

"Okay, Mom," Angie called back.

"That's a terribly expensive saddle," said Kathy from the kitchen.

The frozen supper was from The Gourmet Kitchen in Beverly Hills, where they took credit cards. Angie put it in the microwave and it was done in three minutes. With a book propped in front of her, she sat in the kitchen and ate her dinner alone, having accepted her mother's excuse of a headache. Nick had taken his plate to his room, where he had his own TV.

When Angie was through and had crumpled the elegant tin plate into the compactor, she went outside to the pool and flopped on the big chaise. She lay there a long time, watching an evening mist creep across the tennis court and float softly over the pool.

She thought of calling Gloria, of telling her everything, unloading some of the burden. She thought of Ryan. He wouldn't be back from his school till the end of the week. What was she going to say to Ryan?

The pool phone under the canopy rang loudly, making Angie jump. Raising herself up from the chair, she saw the light in her mother's bedroom go on, and the phone stopped ringing.

She dropped back on the chaise, and after a few minutes the sliding doors to her mother's bedroom opened. "Angie, your dad wants to talk to you."

Angie jumped up and ran to the bench under the canopy. "Daddy . . ."

"Hi, Angie, how's my girl?"

He sounded wonderful, as if he were right there sitting beside her.

"I'm fine, when are you coming home?" she said, making it all sound like one word.

He laughed. "Just as soon as I pick up about a half million dollars."

"Oh, Daddy . . ."

"Listen, honey, I know everything's upside down right this minute, but it's all going to be straightened out, I promise you. Hey, how's Gloria? How's my pal, Edie? And how's Ginger?"

Ginger was Angie's favorite horse at Oakmont.

"She's fine." She took a breath. "Daddy . . ."

"Angie, this is just a temporary roadblock, believe me.

It'll be okay. I'm going to get it cleared up. And listen, this summer you can have your own horse; how about that?''

"I don't need my own horse."

"Sure you do. I've already got you entered in the Malibu show next October."

Angie laughed. "Daddy, you're crazy."

"I know. And I've got to hang up. I'm waiting for a very important call. Love you, honey."

"Daddy . . ."

"Yeah?"

"Are you all right?"

"Of course. Never better."

"Positive?"

"Guarantee."

"Okay, 'night, Daddy. Love you."

" 'Night, Angie. I'll try to call you tomorrow."

She heard him hang up and put the phone down. She sat a long time looking into the pool. She knew it was foolish, but things suddenly felt different. Lighter, more hopeful, simpler. Maybe she'd call Gloria after all, talk about parties or shopping or going to the beach. Or maybe she'd just have a toasted cheese sandwich and go to bed.

Nick was sitting in the kitchen, pouring himself a glass of white wine. She went to the refrigerator, opened it.

"Where's he going to get the dough to give you a horse?" Nick asked.

Angie stiffened. "That was crummy, listening in."

"It was a family call, wasn't it? He's my old man too, isn't he?" He said it sarcastically, as if he didn't care. But he did care. Deep down, he'd always wished he could be easy with Dad, closer, but he didn't know how.

Angie closed the refrigerator, deciding against the snack. She looked at Nick coldly. "You ought to stop drinking; it makes you even nastier than you are."

"You know why he's in Texas, don't you?"

"No, and neither do you."

"I've got a really good guess. It's that classmate of his from Stanford, the one that visited here last year. The guy's wallowing in oil. Dad's going to hit him for enough to bail out Careau Investments."

Nick finished the wine, got up. "It isn't going to work. You're not going to get that horse, Angie. And nobody's going to give a phony like Dad a half a million dollars."

Angie snatched up the wine bottle, aimed it at her brother, but Nick wisely stepped out into the hall and headed for his room.

She put down the bottle and slumped into the kitchen chair. She wanted to put her head down on her arms and let it all out. Tears, crying, the welcome relief of giving in, hitting bottom.

She heard her mother call her name. And she could hear her mother's question before it was spoken. "What did your dad say?"

She couldn't talk to her mother now; she couldn't take it. She ran out the open sliding door. Without missing a step she kicked off her sandals and dived into the pool. She was wearing shorts and a tank top, no drag to the strong crawl that propelled her to the far end of the pool. She swam lap after lap till she saw the light in her mother's bedroom go out. Then she came up the steps and lay stretched out on the diving board, breathing deeply, coming down off the heart-pounding sprint. It was almost as good as crying.

She looked down into the water, lighted from below by a soft blue flood. Slowly, her pulse quieted to normal. It was cool but she didn't feel the touch of the night air. She looked down into the water, thinking, hearing her own voice on that day; was it a hundred years ago? That day she first walked into the new house, and ran back and yelled, "Daddy, it's got a swimming pool!"

*   *   *

A hundred years ago? Well, three years, anyway. She had been thirteen, going on fourteen. It seemed now as if she had never lived in the Valley, as if it were some far off, enchanted place where nobody had any problems, where there were friends who played endlessly on Saturday afternoons, and made weird costumes to go trick or treating on Halloween, and where you knew everybody in school, where the biggest decision of the year was whether to wear eye shadow in class or whether you were falling hopelessly in love with a wickedly sophisticated boy named Teddy who had a 750cc Kawasaki bike and took you for wild rides till Mom found out and broke up the romance by taking you to Europe for three weeks.

That first marvelous trip to Europe wasn't actually to break up the romance with Teddy. It had been one of her father's fantastic ideas. He just came home to the Valley one day with a pile of travel folders about France and said they were all going.

Of course, Mom said he was joking. What would they use for money? And Daddy said you didn't need money. You used little purple-and-brown credit cards. And that's what they did.

Thirteen, going on fourteen. Fabulous, exciting, and then—all of a sudden—scary; their very lives were changing.

There was no getting around it, even when Mom tried to play it down, pretend they were still just folks; Daddy was really making it in business. Angie couldn't get it completely straight, what he really did, but it was kind of glamorous to her. His clients were people you read about in the papers, sometimes show people, the ones you could see on TV. And Daddy made lots of trips to places like Palm Springs and Acapulco.

And he bought himself a bright silver BMW coupe, and everybody on the block knew that the car cost as much as most of the husbands made in a year. Some of Angie's friends got a little cool after the BMW.

Then the thunderbolt, the killer. It snuck in so unexpectedly.

Sometimes, on Sundays, they would go "open housing." Angie kind of liked the game. They'd pile into Mom's station wagon and cruise around till they saw an open-house real estate sign, and they'd go in and look at the house as if they were buyers. It was an innocent amusement and a nice, unsnoopy way of seeing how other people lived.

One open-housing day, Daddy drove over the canyon to Bel-Air. Mom said it was ridiculous, looking at practically million-dollar houses, because the real estate salesperson could tell in a minute they were only looking. Daddy just laughed and said she could stay in the car, which of course, he knew she couldn't.

So the station wagon wound up the high, hedged road, past the tall, iron-gated driveways, and then stopped at a discreet real estate sign.

Daddy seemed to know the real estate person who showed them around. The house, plus a swimming pool and tennis court, was too utterly fabulous.

When they got back in the car, Mom said, "It's beautiful, but I certainly wouldn't want to live in it."

"Why not?" Daddy asked innocently.

Mom shrugged. "I don't know," she answered. "I'd feel uncomfortable. It just isn't me."

Daddy smiled. "You're still Valley, huh?"

"I guess so," Mom said.

So they drove home, and that night after dinner, when Angie went over to Sissie's house to listen to records, Daddy said casually, "I'm going to put a down payment on that house in Bel-Air."

When Angie came home from Sissie's house, the dishes weren't done and she could hear her mother and father in the den. Mom was crying, and Daddy, in this reasonable voice, was saying something like, "We've got to go where the money is, Kathy." And then Mom cried even more.

Three months later they moved into the house in Bel-Air.

Chapter Four

When they first came to the new house, there was no one to talk to, no one to play records with. There were no sidewalks where you could wander out onto your lawn, where someone would come along and invite you down to the boulevard for a Coke or something.

At first Kathy drove Angie back to the Valley for a couple of sleepovers, but it wasn't the same. She was alien now, a rich kid. Even her friend Sissie acted self-conscious, treated her with deference.

And worse. There was talk of sending her to a fancy prep school in Santa Barbara at the end of the summer.

Angie spent a lot of time in the swimming pool, doing endless laps, taking belly-slapping dives off the board. Duke would sit at the end of the board, and she would tell him to watch this one. He watched dutifully, and always thumped his tail triumphantly when she surfaced.

One day, after they had been in the house several weeks, Angie saw a fancy white foreign-looking car in the driveway. It looked like something you might see in an English spy movie, standing in front of a mysteriously abandoned castle.

Dripping from her swim, Angie shuffled back to her room, and there was a woman standing by the window, looking at three samples of fabric spread out on the bed.

41

"Hi," said the woman. "Which one do you like for your bedspread?"

Angie moved to the bed, studied the samples. "I don't know . . . what I mean is . . . I really don't like any of them too much."

The woman smiled. "Neither do I." She held out her hand. "I'm Fran King," she said. And the way she said it implied that Angie ought to know who Fran King was.

Angie did know because Fran King had been the focal point of a hassle between Mom and Dad the first week they were in the house. Daddy had visited a very rich client's house, and the very rich client's wife said that Mom and Dad absolutely had to have Fran King "do" their new house.

Dad found out that anybody who was anybody had his, hers, or their house decorated by Fran King. Stars, heads of aerospace companies, respectable gangsters; Fran "did" everybody. And very rich people felt comfortable in Fran's houses because they knew everything was right, from the big, meaningless abstractions that spewed disorganized color into the living rooms to the exquisite China export pieces, circa 1799, in the dining rooms.

Fran herself was quite decorative. Nobody knew her exact age, somewhere well past thirty-five. She had been a young featured player in a number of films, and had had the good sense to marry out of show business and into big money. After she divorced the big money, she was left with an impressive house in Bel-Air and a taste for nice things. When a friend asked for a little help in choosing the color scheme for her bedroom, Fran discovered her real talent.

"How do you feel about this room?" Fran asked Angie.

"It's too big," Angie said uncertainly. "I get lost."

Fran laughed. "Maybe we could squinch it down a little."

"I liked it the way it used to be. In the old house. But

Mom says all my furniture will have to go, anyway." She looked up at Fran. "Couldn't I keep my rocker? I read in my rocker, it's very . . . comfortable." A sense of desolation, of irrevocable loss washed over Angie.

Fran looked at the rocker. It was small, brown, non-descript, probably bought at a garage sale. But Fran could see it done in stark white with a delicate blue stripe on the arm, and maybe a blue clamshell motif on the back.

"I think we can live with the rocker if we must," Fran said tolerantly.

"Thank you," Angie said. She stood there awkwardly while Fran was decorating the room in her head, becoming suddenly unaware of Angie. After several minutes of this, Angie said, "I think I'd better take off my suit. I'm dripping."

Fran returned from her inner journey. She gathered the samples from the bed. "I think you're going to like the room, Angie."

Angie nodded. But she felt a moment of anger. She wished they'd all leave her room alone. To her it was a kind of last connection to the old, simple life. Her happy life back in the Valley.

Fran smiled a professional smile and left the room to go down the hall to where Mom was studying samples on her bed.

When the final decisions on Angie's room were made, in addition to the rocker she was given a beautiful Eames chair that cost close to a thousand dollars, but mostly she sat on the rocker and gave Duke the new chair, which he really liked more than any place in the house.

Endless afternoons, trips to Beverly Hills for window shopping, then real shopping for clothes to take to Oakmont.

"Why can't I go to public school like everybody else?" Angie asked.

Home briefly from the client wars, Daddy lolled in a chaise under the pool canopy, looked over his drink at

Angie, smiled tenderly. "Because you are not like every-body else. You're special."

"Can I use a vulgar word?" Angie asked.

"No, you're not fourteen yet."

"Well, I'm thinking the word, anyway."

He chuckled. "Okay."

"Daddy . . ."

"Look, baby, Oakmont is the best prep school on the west coast. You can get into any college from there."

"Supposing I don't want to go to any college?"

"Then I'll whack your backside."

She grinned. "You never did."

"I could always start."

"Try it."

He half rose from the chaise. Angie ran to the edge of the pool. He jumped up. She dived in; he dived in after her.

But it wasn't often that Daddy was there to break up the endless afternoons, and when she wasn't shopping or getting out of the way while the rug people and the drape people and the furniture people were transforming the house, she just kind of moped around, dreading the twelfth of September and Oakmont.

She talked to Duke a lot, and since she didn't play tennis and the court was the largest flat space on the grounds, she would often go out there and throw a ball over the net and let Duke chase it.

One day, after Duke got tired chasing the ball, she came off the court and saw a kid in tennis shorts, carrying a racquet and a can of balls, entering the back gate. He was tall, well built, with reddish, curly hair. He looked about seventeen, but actually he was just past fifteen, a year older than Angie.

"Hi," he said with a puzzled smile. "Who are you?"

Angie disliked him instantly. "What do you mean, who am I?"

"I mean, are you visiting here or something?"

"No, I'm not visiting here or something. I live here."

"You live here?"

"Right."

"What happened to Artie?"

"I don't know anyone named Artie."

"Artie Stevens. He owns this house."

"Oh, Mr. Stevens. Well, my father bought this house from Mr. Stevens."

He looked in at the court. "Then there're no regular games on Thursdays and Saturdays?"

"I imagine not," Angie said coolly.

"I always played with Artie on Thursdays and Saturdays. I've been away. Artie's pretty good for fifty-two years old."

"But I'll bet you always beat him."

He grinned. "How did you know?"

"I guessed."

He held out his hand, maintaining the disarming grin. "My name is Ryan." He nodded over his shoulder. "I'm the rich kid who lives at the end of the road, the house with the big iron gates."

She couldn't help taking his hand, even if he was charmingly insufferable. "I'm Angie," she said.

"Hi, Angie."

"Hi."

"You play tennis?"

"No."

"Why not?"

"What do you mean, why not? I just don't play tennis."

"But you've got your own court."

Angie shrugged as if she had always had a court.

"Hey, tell you what, I'll teach you," Ryan said.

"Thanks."

"Where do you go to school?"

"No place, I'm in between. I'm going to Oakmont in September."

"Oakmont," he said with a soft groan.

The groan was too much for Angie. She decided she would either say something devastating or just simply walk away. She couldn't think of anything devastating. "If you'll excuse me," she said. "I have to go in for lunch."

"Lunch? At three o'clock?"

"We eat late," Angie said, with what she figured was a real clincher. "Come on, Duke," she said to the mutt, who had fallen asleep on the nice warm cement of the tennis court.

"Hey, wait a minute. How about a tennis lesson tomorrow, same time?"

"I'm sorry, I'm going shopping."

"Could I use the court to practice serves tomorrow?"

Angie shrugged again. "Help yourself," she said.

"Thanks," said Ryan.

She started toward the house.

"Hey, you really going to Oakmont?"

She stopped. "Yes, I am."

He smiled. "Well, I guess the place could use a little class." He turned and jogged toward the gate. "Be seeing you, Angie."

She watched him go without being able to think of a single punch line that would have cut him down properly.

But the next day when she was shopping with her mother they just happened to pass a sporting goods store, and Angie said maybe she ought to have a tennis racquet, seeing as they had a tennis court. So her mother bought her a racquet, a very nice one, since the store happened to be having a sale.

That afternoon, Angie watched from her room as Ryan practiced serves. She absolutely would not go out there till he was gone, but poor Duke was whining, and, after all, Duke needed to go out.

Ryan's serve was so good and his form so full of life and excitement that Angie just stood there, looking through the gate.

Ryan had placed a tennis ball can in the right hand corner of the service line. With three tries, he knocked the can right off the court.

"Wow!" Angie yelled in spite of herself.

Ryan turned. "Oh, hi," he called. "I'm serving."

"Yeah, I can see," Angie said.

"Where's your racquet?" he asked, coming to the gate.

"Well . . ." Angie stalled.

"Go on, get your racquet, we'll have a lesson."

She ran into the house and grabbed the racquet.

When she got on the court, Ryan became totally serious. "Okay," he said, "here's your first position."

Angie thought they'd hit the ball and have fun, but all she did for almost an hour was face the net, then turn sideways, then bring the racquet back, then shift her weight and follow through. No ball, no running, nothing. She was exhausted.

"You've got nice coordination," Ryan commented.

"Thanks," Angie said. "Can I sit down?"

They sat under the canopy.

"Would you like a Coke?" Angie asked.

Ryan nodded.

She went to the small refrigerator behind the outside bar. They sat with the Cokes, cooling off, and then Ryan said, "You want to meet my grandmother?"

"Your grandmother?" Angie thought that was probably the weirdest proposition she had ever had.

"Yeah, Nan." He laughed. "I stopped calling her Nana when I was seven. She'd like to meet you. I told her all about you."

Angie shook her head, bewildered. "How could you tell her all about me? You don't know anything about me."

He smiled. "I could learn."

"Well, really . . . why would your grandmother . . ."

"Come on, it's not far. We can ride our bikes."

"No, I can't."

"You have to have lunch, huh?"

She laughed.

"Some other time then?" he asked.

"That would be better."

He stood up. "Well, I guess I'd better go."

Angie stood up.

He leaned toward her, touched her chin with his fist, and kissed her very lightly on the forehead.

"Be seeing you, Angie. Same time tomorrow."

She just stood there, watching him run toward the outside gate. He stopped, patted Duke, waved to her, and was gone.

Angie sat down on the chaise. Duke came shuffling up to have his ears scratched. She scratched Duke fondly and wondered how she could ever wait through the next twenty-four hours.

Angie had never realized what a great game tennis was. And on her own court. Up until Ryan, the court was only a place to throw balls to Duke. But now it took on a new dimension. She had to be honest with herself; the court had snob appeal. It was really a blatant status symbol, like having a camper that slept four in your driveway in the Valley.

Having money had its points, Angie suddenly realized. And when Daddy arranged for her to use her own credit card, she bought designer jeans, a half-dozen signature tennis outfits, a fancy new collar for Duke.

And there was something else that money gave her. It was a heady, indefinable feeling of power, of command, to say airily—as if she had been doing it all her life— "Charge it, please." They were more than ordinary words;

they were an incantation. "Abracadabra . . . Open sesame
. . . Charge it, please."

The little plastic credit card was the amulet; the enchanted good-luck charm; the magic wand, which when
waved could give her anything her heart desired: the fabled
three wondrous wishes; the golden eggs; the fairyland
castle; the magic carpet; the handsome prince.

The Valley seemed so far away now; only months, but it
seemed like years. She could imagine meeting that snotty
Ruthie Bonner, who lived two houses down the block back
in the Valley—Ruthie was a tennis buff—and saying to
Ruthie, "Would you like to play on my court today?"
And Ruthie staring at her, wide-eyed, and saying, "You
have your own court?" And Angie trying to keep the smug
look off her own face. Oh, that stuck-up Ruthie would
really hate her now.

And it wasn't only the tennis court; it was the whole
new way of looking at things. Never asking how much
something cost, just charging it. Her mother could never
get over that.

There were arguments. Daddy would say, buy it, whatever it was. And Mom would say, can we afford it? And
he'd get mad, as if she were questioning his manhood or
something.

Nick, of course, wallowed deliciously in the new setup.
He hit Daddy for a sports car and took up golf so he could
join the Hidden Knolls Country Club. The Club had tennis
courts too, and Nick played at the Club, reaching the
ultimate in conspicuous consumption, having his own court
and paying to play somewhere else.

The whole thing took on a crazy kind of momentum.
The parties, for instance. As soon as Fran King had the
house decorated in familiar variations of all her other
houses, they began to give parties. The parties were a
great strain on Mom, but she knew they were essential to
Daddy's business. And Fran always helped with the guest

list, so there were lots of show people, the successful ones, and aerospace people, and even someone who owned a race horse that had won almost a million dollars in one season. Angie smiled at that one. In Bel-Air even the horses were in the top tax bracket.

The party to show off the new abstraction that Fran had persuaded Daddy to buy was the worst party ever. The picture was a series of slashes of blood-red on black, with a pink gob in one corner. The guests were sure to love it since a number of them had similar gobs by the same artist.

"I hate that picture," said Kathy in a tense, low voice as she came out of her huge dressing room, a gown hanging over her arm.

Her mother stood in front of her vanity table while Angie helped her get her dress over her head without mussing Kathy's hairdo.

"It is pretty awful," Angie said.

"But they'll love it; I know they will," Kathy said. She looked up as if seeing the picture. "It says something important, doesn't it?" she said acidly.

Angie laughed.

"It isn't funny, Angie."

"I know." Angie opened Kathy's jewel box, held up a pair of earrings. "These'd go nice."

"It isn't just that awful picture," Kathy said bitterly.

"Mom, simmer down," Angie said gently.

Kathy took a deep breath. "I'm sorry, baby."

"It's only something on the wall."

"I know, I know. And it's only a party and it'll be over soon enough." She straightened the dress, turned to Angie.

"Oh, Mom, you look so beautiful, it's disgusting."

Kathy laughed and gave her a quick hug. Angie handed her the earrings.

"Oh dear," Kathy said. "I almost forgot. The scarf that

goes with the dress. Find it, will you, Angie? It's some-place in one of the drawers in the dressing room.''

Angie went into the dressing room, opened the top drawer built in beside the door. She heard Daddy come into the bedroom. "The catering lady is all set up," he said to Kathy. "She wants to know when you want to serve the canapés."

"Why don't you ask Fran?" Kathy said nervously.

Angie stopped looking for the scarf. She just stood there.

"Fran isn't here yet," Daddy said quietly.

"It's really her party. Ask her." Kathy said.

"Never mind that. Let me look at you." Angie heard her father say. Then he whistled. "Gorgeous!" he said. "Come on, let's get ready to greet our friends."

Angie was about to leave the dressing room, but stopped at her mother's quiet words. "They're not our friends."

"Of course they are," Daddy laughed. "Let's go. I'll mix you a stiff pre-party drink for your pre-party nerves."

"It's all wrong," Kathy said.

"It's lovely. Smashing."

"I don't mean the dress," Angie's mother said edgily.

"Then what?"

There was a moment of silence, then Kathy said, "The people, your clients, prospective customers; we hardly know them."

"Relax, honey, it's only a party," Daddy said soothingly.

"A glorified business meeting. Not a party." Mom paused. Then: "Oh, Jim, what's the sense of it? This . . . this performance? This show?"

"Kathy, Kathy, sure it's partly show. Look, baby, the parties, meeting the right people. It's all part of the game, part of being successful, getting to the top. You can see what it's done for us."

"I hate it, Jim. I hate what it's done for us. Parties used to be fun, close friends. I hate what it's done to the children. Angie, lonely, missing her old friends, pretending she doesn't feel out of place . . ."

Angie stiffened. Mom must have forgotten Angie was there. Should she show hereslf? But Mom went on: ". . . and Nick. Nick's become an unbearable snob. And me, I don't belong in this . . ." She let the sentence trail off.

"Kathy, honey, you're exaggerating," Daddy answered. "You're a little scared, that's all. Lots of people let success frighten them. You'll get used to it. You'll love it one day, believe me."

"You're not listening, Jim. You haven't heard a word I've said. We don't talk anymore. You've forgotten who I am."

There was stillness now. Angie peeked around the door. Her father had Kathy in his arms.

Angie drew back. She couldn't interrupt them now.

"You're my love," Daddy said. "I need you."

Then her mother, her voice breaking: "Oh, Jim, Jim, I love you so much."

Angie could picture the two of them embracing. Then, finally, her father said, "We'd better go."

"You go ahead. I have to fix my makeup," Kathy answered.

Angie heard Daddy leave the room. She took her time finding the scarf.

When she came back into the bedroom, she saw her mother through the open door of the bathroom.

Kathy was standing before the medicine cabinet. She opened it with trembling hands and took out a vial of Valium.

She shook two tablets out and gulped them down with a glass of water.

Chapter Five

It was the day before Angie had to go to Oakmont. To add to her apprehension, it was raining. She felt awful. She stood in the middle of the room, with a terrible mess of clothes that she was supposed to pack.

The telephone rang. She looked at the clock. Nine thirty. She knew who it was. He called every morning at the same time. It had gotten so that her mother sometimes picked up the phone and handed it to her without even listening, and said, "It's Ryan."

Angie picked up the phone in her room.

"Hi," Ryan said in a subdued voice.

"Hi," Angie answered, even more subdued.

"What are you doing?"

"Nothing. Packing."

"Oh. Packing."

"You want to come over?" Angie asked.

"It's raining."

"I know."

"I'll be over," Ryan said.

"Okay."

She put down the phone, sat on the bed, and looked at her scattered clothes. How could she leave Ryan?

After that first tennis lesson, he came over every day. And without saying much about it, they became aware that something important had happened, that each of them was somebody new when they were with each other.

And there was no peer pressure; they were almost alone for the summer. There was no pressure to make a commitment, or to go to wild parties; no pressure about booze and pot and all the peer traps that demanded surrender of their values.

They could discover themselves and each other slowly. It was a summer not to be forgotten.

And Angie met Ryan's grandmother. That was something else.

Ryan's grandmother lived at the Bel-Haven Hotel in Bel-Air. She had a 1932 Type J Duesenberg, which she drove herself and showed at classic car meets. In the thirties, she had been one of the most photographed women in the country. She had been divorced four times, and she couldn't stand her daughter, Ryan's mother, who she thought was a terrible snob . . . which was true. And Grandmother was sorry for Ryan's father, who had inherited millions and didn't have anything better to do than make more millions.

Grandmother rarely visited Ryan's home. She showed up only for weddings and funerals. She had been there for the wedding of Ryan's older sister and had criticized the champagne and her daughter's dress, which she said was revoltingly matronly.

But she loved Ryan.

So one afternoon, Angie and Ryan biked to the hotel to have lunch with Nan. The headwaiter seated them at a lovely corner table and said Mrs. Halley would be there soon, and served them each a fantastic shrimp cocktail for starters.

When Nan appeared there was an immediate flutter of waiters, and several heads turned and whispered her name.

Nan was approaching seventy, with no intention of ever

arriving there. She was still a beautiful woman, with just a slight tuck behind the ears to gently lift the perfect face.

Ryan stood up and kissed her.

She sat and took Angie's hand. "How's the shrimp?" she asked Angie.

"Very good," Angie said.

Nan turned to the waiter and ordered shrimp and a very dry martini. She took Ryan's hand too.

"This is nice," she said. "I've been wanting to meet Angie."

"What did I tell you?" Ryan said, looking at Angie proudly.

Nan smiled at Angie. "You were right."

"And she's smart too," Ryan said.

"I can see that," Nan laughed.

Angie squirmed a little but managed to smile.

"How's her tennis?" Nan asked.

"Terrible," Ryan said.

"Good," said Nan. "It builds too many leg muscles."

"But she swims twenty laps every day."

"So do I," Nan said.

"You do!" Angie exclaimed. "That's wonderful!"

"At my age," Nan said dryly.

Angie laughed. "Oh no, I meant well, you look so . . ."

"Well preserved." Nan smiled. "Well, I am, my dear."

"A monument to the cosmetics industry," Ryan grinned.

"Ryan, really," Angie said reprovingly.

"It's all right," said Nan. "He's an ill-mannered child, and I'm cutting him out of my will as of this moment." She leaned over and kissed Ryan on the top of the head. "What are you two doing this afternoon?"

"We're going to the movies with you, Nan."

"Oh," Nan said, "what are we seeing?"

"*Space Monsters*. You'll love it," Ryan said.

"You don't have to go if you don't want to, Mrs. Halley," Angie said. Then to Ryan: "Please, Ryan . . ."

"Oh, I have to go," Nan said. "The child has me under his thumb. A terrible tyrant."

They looked at each other, Ryan and Nan, and smiled. The tenderness between them included Angie, drawing her into a circle of warm delight. It was a wonderful day, meeting Nan.

The twelfth of September, and they had driven the ninety miles up the coast highway, mostly in silence, and now they were entering the road that led to Oakmont School.

Angie felt it was the road to oblivion. She had spent a smoggy, desolate farewell day with Ryan. And now the sun was shining on a burst of climbing red trumpet vine that covered the gateposts of Oakmont. But Angie felt she was at the bottom of the pits.

"Well, here we are," Daddy said cheerfully.

And Mom, in the back seat, said, "Oh, it's so beautiful."

And Angie looked straight ahead, saying nothing but thinking: Who would her roommates be? Supposing they were just awful? Supposing they were snobs and were overdressed and came from the best families? Supposing they saw right through her, that she was just an awkward kid from the Valley and didn't really belong in all this high-class splendor?

And they were sure to have a language all their own, with words that were in and words that were out, and if you didn't know which were which you were sunk.

Of course, they'd all know how to ride much better than she did. And supposing her britches and cap were wrong? And supposing Ryan didn't write? He just had to! They had promised each other. A letter a day. Or at least every other day. That might make it bearable for Angie.

So what if she had terrible roommates, and they talked some weird jargon? At least, no matter what, she'd have Ryan's letters. If he wrote, that is.

Daddy stopped the car at the top of the hill. They could see the whole school and the ocean below. It was spectacular. But all Angie saw was the dashboard clock. In less than an hour she'd be here alone. Abandoned, deserted, alone.

There were half a dozen cars in the parking area. Girls, baggage, parents. Girls jumping out of cars, calling names, squealing with delight, hugging old friends, grabbing luggage, running wildly into the dorms.

Angie very slowly got out of the car. She knew her way around, having spent several hours at the school when she came with Mom to look it over.

"Why don't you take your stuff up to your room?" Daddy said. "Mom and I have business in the front office."

Angie picked up her bags.

"We'll be up later, dear," Mom said.

Angie nodded listlessly and entered the dorm. She almost got mowed down by a gaggle of sophomores rushing down the stairs, screeching inanities and laughing raucously.

Angie knew the names of her roommates, which were posted along with hers on the door. Gloria Henning, Edith Riker.

Gloria, she knew, would be in her class; Edith, a grade higher.

Angie dropped her suitcase and looked at the room. It was adequate, functional. Three beds, three desks, a large closet. But there were bright posters on the wall, and two of the beds were already made up with colorful bedspreads. Edie's, a raffish Indian print; Gloria's, a fabulous old-fashioned quilt.

There was a typewriter on one of the desks where Angie was standing. She looked out the window at the students milling in the courtyard below, then, idly, she tapped several keys on the typewriter.

"Don't touch that!" said a sharp voice.

Angie lifted her fingers as if she had been scalded. She turned around.

Edie marched into the room. "Nobody . . . but absolutely nobody touches that typewriter. Okay?"

"I'm terribly sorry!" Angie apologized.

Edie put the cover on the typewriter. "I worked one whole summer for that machine." She held out her hand. "I'm Edie. You're Angie, huh?"

Angie nodded. "I'm really sorry . . ."

"It's okay," Edie said. "We've got a zone system in this room. No-touch areas."

"Yes, I understand," Angie said miserably.

Edie crossed to the closet, opened it. "This end is yours."

Angie nodded again. "Thank you," she said just above a whisper.

"You want me to help you unpack?"

"No. That's okay. I can manage."

Edie sat on the bed. "All right, I'll watch."

Angie looked puzzled.

Now Edie smiled. "I want to see if you've got anything that'll fit me. I can't wear Gloria's stuff, she's too tall."

Angie looked closely at Edie. They were about the same size but Edie was kind of muscular, stocky almost. She wasn't pretty, but her firm, intelligent face, topped by a mop of black, unruly hair, gave out a feeling of great animation.

Angie put her suitcase on the bed and unzipped the top. She took out a beautiful pale blue cashmere sweater.

"Ah . . ." Edie said.

Angie took out a pair of tailored jeans.

Edie grinned. "Those'd be too tight in the seat." She looked up at someone standing in the doorway.

Angie turned to see Gloria. And Angie's heart sank to the bottom. Even at fourteen, Gloria was so lovely it was revolting.

"Hi," Edie said to Gloria. She nodded toward Angie. "This is Angie. Angie, Gloria."

Gloria came in with a smile, holding out her hand. "Hi." she said.

Angie took the hand and answered almost inaudibly.

Edie picked up the sweater, held it in front of her. "How would I look in this?"

"Terrible," Gloria said. "It's not your color."

"So what's my color?"

"Green. To go with those cat's eyes."

Edie laughed. "She doesn't mean it. She's really scared I'm going to beat her out for beauty queen." She picked up a bright red blouse, continued to Gloria: "Everything pretty sweaty down there?"

Angie knew it. They had their personal school language. Sweaty was probably an in word, something everybody on campus would know. She felt more and more miserable. Alien, not wanted, an intruder. How was she ever going to make it till Christmas?

". . . riding?" Gloria asked.

Angie had missed the first part of the sentence. "What?"

"Are you signing up for riding?"

"Yes, I think so."

"Good. Don't let them sell you Dixie. She's barn happy."

Whatever that meant, thought Angie. Desperately, she turned to Edie. "Do you ride?"

"Me?" Edie grinned. "No money. I'm here on scholarship."

"Oh," Angie said.

"I'm the token intellectual. There's one of us in each form. We look good on the school brochures, and we bring up the SAT scores."

A beauty queen and a token intellectual. Now Angie knew she wasn't going to make it till Christmas.

Then Daddy poked his head in the door. "Hi," he said.

"Your mom's haggling over the bed linen charge. I had to get out." He stepped into the room, smiling. "It says Gloria and Edie on the door."

Gloria pointed to herself. "Gloria."

He held out his hand. "Hi, Gloria."

Then he took Edie's hand and said hi to her. But the hi was very warm and friendly. He turned to Angie. "Scared stiff, honey?"

Angie was embarrassed.

He laughed. "Freshman year, my roommate was a towering football hulk. He terrified me till I found out he was allergic to cats."

Edie laughed. "We get the message."

"Good," he said. "Where's the fanciest place you eat lunch in Santa Barbara?"

"The Mill Road Tavern," Gloria said.

"They rob you," Edie added.

"Fine," he said. "How about the three of us and Angie's mom getting robbed for lunch?"

"We'd need permission," Gloria hesitated.

"It's okay," Daddy said. "I've been charming the management."

"You've been charming Miss Storey?" Edie asked in wonderment.

"Not easy," he laughed. "But I can be pretty irresistible."

"Daddy, please . . ." Angie was devastated.

Edie laughed. "You are convincing, Mr. . . ."

"Careau."

"Mr. Careau. We accept with extreme pleasure."

"Okay, let's go," he said.

Angie knew he had a business appointment back in Los Angeles in the early afternoon, and he wasn't going to make it. He smiled and put his arm around her waist as they went down the stairs.

The lunch was a success. The girls loved Daddy and soon were including Angie in jokes about manners, customs, and morals on the campus. She found that sweaty meant confused. And barn happy was a horse that always headed for home. And she learned other words that were current in the hidden vocabulary.

The lunch wasn't over till two. Daddy's day was shot. But Angie hoped her good-bye hug and kiss, before she went into the dorm, expressed to him how much it meant to her.

That night Angie unpacked fully. Last of all, she put Ryan's picture on her desk.

Edie, in her robe, came in from the down-hall bath and saw it first.

"Wow!" Edie exclaimed.

"His name is Ryan."

"Hey, Gloria . . ."

Gloria rolled over in bed.

"Look what Angie's got."

"His name is Ryan," Angie repeated.

Gloria sat up, put on her glasses. "Oh, he's lovely."

"Men aren't lovely," Edie said. "They're handsome or sexy. . . ."

"He's lovely," Gloria said and rolled back in bed. " 'Night, Edie, Angie."

Edie sighed. "She's telling us to get to bed. 'Night, Gloria."

"Good night," Angie said. She got into bed, and Edie turned out the lights.

Angie took a deep breath, exhaled slowly, and lay back on her pillow. She decided she was going to make it till Christmas.

It wasn't like a prison at all. At the end of the first week, it felt as if she had been coming to Oakmont for years. Mostly because of Gloria.

Everybody loved Gloria; everybody protected her. Gloria was incredibly beautiful, but she couldn't stay on a horse. On the basketball court, she'd trip even when no one was near her. And if a lunch tray crashed to the floor in the dining room, nobody even turned around to see who had goofed. They knew it was Gloria.

Angie had never met anyone like Gloria. The girl who had everything and spilled most of everything on her new dress. Gloria had a terrific laugh, and she could laugh at herself most of all. Angie thought she was wonderful and wanted to protect her too. Angie didn't realize that Gloria was protecting her, Angie, against the covert slights and exclusions that were usually visited on a new girl.

And, of course, there was Edie. Angie liked her, but Edie was more remote at first, a little defensive. Being on scholarship, she was aware of the money gap between her and the other girls. Gloria was totally unaware of money. When she had it, she spent it on friends or lost it. Most times, she lost it.

The first weeks were a wild, exciting jumble. And just a little scary. Oakmont was serious about college. There were no easy grades, no soft courses, no undemanding teachers. But when Angie started to founder in first year Latin, Edie grabbed hold and held her head above the classical flood.

"*A, ab, absque* . . . what do they do?" Edie drilled at her.

"Take the ablative," Angie said wearily at twelve o'clock on the night before the quiz.

In her bed, Gloria yawned loudly. "I'm asleep. Doesn't anybody care?"

"*Corum, cum, de* . . ." Edie went on relentlessly. "What's next?"

"Sine, pro, prae . . ." Angie mumbled.

So she aced the quiz, and was so pleased she took both girls to lunch at the Mill Road Tavern and put the tab on the credit card that Daddy had given her for "emergencies." It was a memorable day.

And there were the letters. The long, newsy ones she wrote endlessly to Ryan, and the skimpy notes she got back. But they were highly satisfactory because they always ended with "Love, Ryan." Ryan! He could have just sent the one word and that would have been enough.

Chapter Six

Before she caught her breath, it was Christmas vacation. When she came home bursting with stories of Oakmont, her wonderful roommates, and a respectable grade average, no one was more pleased than Daddy.

Nick, of course, said that Oakmont stank.

"Why?" Angie asked.

He shrugged. It wasn't worth explaining. Nick was going to a private school whose inmates rated girls' schools on a rigid social ladder where the bottom rung was scholastic achievement.

But Nick couldn't spoil Angie's vacation because Ryan appeared on the second morning she was home, and every morning thereafter until Christmas day when he waited till afternoon to give her the present—a lovely coral necklace—that, he confessed, Nan had helped pick out for him.

The thing with Ryan was just about perfect. They didn't even have to talk if they didn't feel like it. They'd take long walks, arms around each other's waists, heads together; walks up in the hills above Ryan's house. They passed his house a number of times. Angie didn't ask why they never went in.

One day he told her. "You wouldn't like my mother."

"How do you know?"

He shrugged. "You just wouldn't."

"But how do you know?" she persisted.

"Let's not talk about it," he said.

So they walked in silence for a while.

"Is she mean?" Angie asked.

"No."

"Then what?"

He stopped, looked up at the hills. "When you first moved in, she asked me, 'Who are they?' "

"Who are we?"

"Yeah. Where do you come from? Are you good family?"

"What's good family?"

"I don't know."

"You know, Ryan."

"Okay. A good family has money from way back. Old money. Like if your great-grandfather was a crooked railroad builder, and stole government land, and piled up a bloody fortune, that's pretty old money. Real old money is what they stole from the Indians."

Angie smiled. "I guess we're not old money."

"You just wouldn't like her."

"Do you?"

"She's my mother."

They walked in silence some more. It was just a little cold, and the sky was overcast as it often was in December. It even looked like rain.

"Maybe we'd better go back," Ryan said.

"I like walking in the rain."

He laughed and shook his head wryly. "I'll bet you never walked in the rain. You probably got the idea out of a book."

She laughed too. "Well, I could try it."

He looked up at the sky. "We're not going to have any choice."

In a few minutes it began to rain lightly. They walked faster. Then it came down hard. They ran.

They came to the road and the iron gates in front of Ryan's house. He pushed the gates open and pulled her in. They ran up the driveway to the marble-columned porte cochere in front of the house.

Angie had only seen the place from the gates. Now, she took in the size and grandeur. The front was stark white marble with a gray-blue slate roof and tall arched windows below. It had been built in the twenties for a film producer by an English architect. The word *house* was inadequate; it was by any definition, a mansion.

Breathless and laughing, they stood under the shelter of the porte cochere.

"You're soaked," Ryan said. "Come on." He opened the heavy oak doors, ringing the doorbell at the same time. Both dripping, they stood in the entryway. Angie barely had time to look at the large living room when an elderly woman came toward them.

"Hi, Cora," Ryan said. "This is Miss Careau. Can you take care of her, please?"

Cora answered impassively. "Yes, sir."

"Let her take a shower in the guest room and put her clothes in the dryer, okay?"

Cora nodded.

"Is Mother home?"

"No, sir, she's gone to the Garden Club meeting."

"Okay." He touched Angie on the shoulder. "Go along with Cora."

Angie looked dubious. "It's not far to my house . . ." she began.

"Go on, go on! Get those wet clothes off."

Angie followed Cora through the living room. It was obvious from a quick glance that Fran King hadn't done this house. There were simple but elegant antiques and a huge Persian rug on the floor. The furniture looked comfortable and lived in. The fireplace, in spite of its bulk, gave a feeling of warmth to the room.

The guest room was charming, its size tamed by soft drapes and a graceful chaise in front of the large, floor-length window.

Cora set out towels and a bathrobe. Angie smiled her thanks. She slipped out of her wet clothes and handed them out the door of the bathroom.

The hot shower felt marvelous. She wanted to stay in for hours despite a small uneasy feeling that said maybe she ought to be somewhere else.

But she stayed under the water for ages. Finally, she stepped out and put on the bathrobe. It was pale yellow quilted satin, just about her size. She didn't even ask herself how that was possible. Evidently things were arranged differently in white marble mansions.

Angie opened the bathroom door. Ryan was sitting on the big upholstered chair opposite the chaise, and there were two cups of coffee and some small cakes on a serving table.

Ryan had put on a thick terry cloth robe, but his bare feet were sunk comfortably into the heavy carpet.

"That felt good, huh?" He smiled warmly.

Angie returned the smile. "I didn't want to get out of the shower, ever. It must be imported water or something."

"Comes by caravan from Palm Springs."

Angie laughed and plopped down luxuriously on the chaise. Ryan handed her a cup of coffee.

She sipped the steaming coffee. "Mmm," she sighed.

Ryan sipped his coffee, looked over the rim of the cup at her. "You know something, you're so beautiful, it's nauseating."

"Stop it, Ryan."

"Okay."

She laughed. "No, go ahead."

"Uh-uh, you don't appreciate it."

"Oh, I do, I do. Say something else."

He smiled, took her hand.

"That's nice," she said.

He leaned across the small table, brushed her damp hair with his lips. "You're still sopping," he said softly.

"Mmm, tell me more."

He laughed, sank back in his chair. There was a knock on the door. "Okay, Cora," he called. "Come in." But it wasn't Cora. It was his mother.

Ryan got up quickly. "Hi," he said to his mother. "This is Angela, Mother. We got caught in the rain and I made her take a shower. Cora's drying her clothes. Angie, this is my mother."

Angie had already gotten up.

Mrs. Cleland came across the room in a few steps. She wasn't smiling.

"I seem to have come home at the wrong time, Ryan."

"Mother . . ."

"I suggest you put on some proper clothes. I'll visit with Angela if I may."

"Mother, we really did get caught in the rain . . ."

"Ryan, put on some clothes. And please do not walk around the house in bare feet."

"Yes, ma'am," Ryan said. He gave Angie a glance of commiseration. "I'll see if Cora's got your clothes, Angie."

Painfully aware of her lack of clothing under the bathrobe, Angie sat on the edge of the chaise.

"I'm not going to ask impertinent questions," Evelyn Cleland began. "I presume you *were* caught in the rain . . . if Ryan says so."

"I'm terribly sorry," Angie said. "I told Ryan I could run down to my house—"

"Ryan," Evelyn said, cutting her off, "tends to be impulsive." She smiled very thinly. "I imagine you've noticed that."

Angie opened her mouth to speak but Evelyn went on: "We do not, of course, like to monitor his friends but this is, after all, an impressionable age, isn't it?"

Angie didn't know what to say. She tucked her bare feet under the bathrobe.

"How old are you, my dear?"

"I'll be fifteen in June."

"You're very fond of Ryan."

"We . . . we're good friends."

Evelyn looked pointedly at the bathrobe. "Yes, that's obvious."

Angie felt her cheeks burn. "No, Mrs. Cleland, I think you've got it wrong . . ."

Evelyn cut her off again. "My dear, I don't need explanations." She stood up. "Relationships between young people have changed, I understand that. But they have not changed in this house." She walked to the door, turned to face Angie. "I have plans for Ryan, Angela. I don't want him to be involved beyond his depth at this time." Again the smile that wasn't a smile. "Do finish your coffee. I'm glad we had a chance for a little chat."

Numbly, Angie stood watching her go, hardly believing the words she had just heard.

Holding her clothes and a pair of dry sneakers, Ryan opened the door. He dropped the stuff on the bed and took Angie in his arms.

"Okay, okay," he said softly. "I can guess what she said."

Angie fought back tears.

He held her at arm's length. "Look, Angie, it doesn't matter what she said. What matters is you and me, right?"

Angie buried her head in his shoulder.

"Angie, are you going to make me say it? You know how I hate to say it. You say it for both of us."

"I do love you, Ryan."

He took a deep breath. "That's better."

She moved back from him. "I'll get dressed." She saw the sneakers on the bed. "I'll float in those awful sneakers of yours."

"I can carry you home."

"I'd like that."

He laughed. "Get dressed."

Angie picked up the clothes, smiled wryly. "Well, I met your mother."

He returned the smile. "It's just you and me, Angie. Don't ever forget it."

When Angie opened her eyes in the morning, she sighed luxuriously. Mmmm . . . no school. Vacation.

Then she stiffened as ugly fragments of yesterday rushed in on her: school, Mom's disjointed call . . . Careau Investments . . . that number has been disconnected . . . Nick . . . Dad in trouble, real trouble . . . Texas . . . Daddy's voice: It'll be okay, I promise you . . . I promise you . . . I promise you. . . .

Angie sighed heavily. She didn't want to get up. She couldn't face the frightened look in her mother's eyes. She refused to hear any more of Nick's barbed snipes against Dad. Daddy. His voice on the telephone last night had sounded so reassuring, as if nothing terrible were happening, as if buying her a horse of her own were the most important thing on his mind.

Daddy. Well, of course Daddy would straighten everything out. He'd never lied to her before; he wouldn't lie now. If it were serious, he'd say so. Mom was only overreacting. And Nick? Nick always got his kicks out of scaring Angie. Nothing so new about that. Yet Angie burrowed deeper into her covers, consciously blocked out her thoughts.

But then her telephone began to ring. She tried to ignore it, pulled her pillow over her head. It was probably only Gloria or Edie asking what the plot of the day was to be. The phone stopped ringing. Relieved, Angie rolled over, tried to float back into sleep. An instant later the phone started up again. She picked it up on the sixth ring.

Before Angie said hello, Gloria began speaking: "Come on, get out of the sack, we've got a big day ahead of us."

"Gloria, I don't think . . ."

"You're not supposed to think! This is vacation, remember? Listen, we're having brunch at the Club; then we're hauling Edie down to Venice; then we're going to . . ."

Angie could hear Edie's voice in the background.

"Listen, Gloria," Angie said, "I can't . . ."

But Gloria went on: "Edie says she accidentally put your blue silk blouse back in your side of the closet and she wants to borrow it back, so bring it along to the Club, okay?"

"I'm trying to tell you, I have to stay home."

"What for?"

How could Angie tell her she needed to be alone today? That there was a crisis in the family, that she was in the pits, that she wasn't in the mood for fun and games, that she had to be by the phone in case Daddy called again. . . .

"Angie?" Gloria said. "Angie, you there?"

"I'm here."

Gloria laughed. "Well wake up, we'll see you at eleven. Don't be late, we're starving."

Then Edie's voice over Gloria's last words: "And don't forget to bring the blouse."

Then the phone went dead.

Angie sighed. Maybe she was the one who was overreacting. She got out of bed and started for the shower. Sure, it would all be okay. Daddy had promised.

The Hidden Knolls Country Club lived up to its name. It pretended, to the passing traffic, that it wasn't there. Its roadside frontage camouflaged its park-like acres by huge eucalyptus trees. A discreet brass-plated sign at the security guarded gatehouse behind ornate wrought iron never hinted at the vast, luxurious complex behind it. To the uninformed, the Club entrance was just another private Bel-Air estate.

On the short drive to the Club, Angie and her mother exchanged few words. Kathy seemed preoccupied, vaguely mentioned something about an appointment in Beverly Hills. And Angie, having decided to meet them, was beginning to look forward to seeing Gloria and Edie.

Angie was hungry. The Club was famous for its eggs Benedict, cooked to order by Henri, the imported French chef. But Angie always succumbed to the sumptuous buffet with its artistically arranged dishes—a real production— surrounded by tropical fruits and colorful, exotic fresh flowers.

At the entrance to the dining room, Angie was greeted with a half bow by the maître d'. He nodded across the room toward the latticed patio. "Miss Careau," he said formally, "your friends are waiting in the east terrace."

"Thank you, Jules," Angie said as she spotted Gloria and Edie at an outdoor table.

Angie crossed the large room, the tempting scent of strong coffee and good food hurrying her along. Passing the long, beautifully laden buffet table, she knew that again the eggs Benedict were out. Who could resist the kiwi fruit and all the other surprises on the carefully designed buffet?

"Did you bring it?" Edie asked as Angie took her seat and the waiter simultaneously poured her coffee.

"Bring what?"

"The blouse. You didn't forget?"

Angie pulled a plastic bag out of her purse, tossed it to Edie.

"Thanks," Edie smiled.

"Edie's having the eggs Benedict. I'm for the buffet," Gloria said. "How about you?"

"Buffet," Angie said to the waiter. She took a sip of her coffee. It was marvelous, as usual.

"Hey, is Nick home yet?" asked Edie.

Angie nodded, pulled a face.

"I think he's cute," Edie said.

"He's miserable, as usual."

"Yeah, but he's rich," cracked Edie. "Why don't you fix me up, Angie? With my brains and his money, we'd make a perfect match."

Angie laughed as she rose to go to the buffet. "Come on, Gloria, let's get some food." The coffee had stimulated her appetite; she was with her friends; her mood lightened.

While the girls ate, Gloria and Edie filled Angie in on some of the plans they had made last night. Angie went along with all of them, smiling, nodding, ignoring the niggling thoughts that kept surfacing: What about Daddy? Supposing Nick was right? What if . . . But gradually, the fabulous food, the intimate chatter, the matchless coffee dispelled all the worries. She let herself be swept into the crazy, giggling high of the vacation possibilities, the party at Gloria's, the sleepover at Edie's, the reunion with Ryan.

Finally Edie, who had polished off her own plate and was picking at some of the fruit on Angie's, leaned back and said, "My mother said she'd have a big dinner waiting for us." She laughed indulgently. "But she probably forgot she said it even before she hung up. We'd better go, though. My dad told me to be home by two."

Expertly reading signs of departure, the waiter, carrying the bill on a silver tray, was instantly at the table. "I'll sign it," Angie said. "It's my turn."

"No, my treat," Gloria insisted. But as she reached out, she knocked over her cup of coffee and some of it spilled onto her jeans. "Oh, no!" she moaned.

"Klutz!" Edie said, laughing. "We just can't take you anywhere!"

In dismay, Gloria looked down at herself. The coffee had made a large dark stain on the front of her pants. "I'm

going to the restroom. Walk in front of me, okay, Edie?"
she asked, blushing.

"You two go ahead, I'll take care of the bill," Angie
said.

Angie signed the bill and the waiter moved off. She
sipped at her coffee and smiled. Poor Gloria. She *was* a
klutz.

But that was part of her appeal. Just as you began to
suspect she was too perfect to be human, she'd pull something like this. Angie'd never forget the freshman tea when
Gloria was chosen to pour. She poured, all right. She
poured quite beautifully, the picture of the gracious socialite,
poised, lovely, composed. Until she accidentally poured
past the cup and onto the hand of the dean of women from
a neighboring school. Gloria had lost her contact lenses
and was not wearing her glasses. She . . .

"Miss Careau?"

Angie looked up. The waiter was standing at her elbow,
the silver tray in his hand. He leaned over and very quietly
said, "I'm sorry, we can no longer accept your signature."

"I don't understand," Angie said. And then it hit her.
She understood. "Wait a minute," she said as she began
to rummage around in her purse. "I'll pay cash." But she
knew she didn't have the fifty-two dollars plus tip that the
breakfast had cost. Embarrassed, she pulled out a single
twenty-dollar bill. Sometimes she stashed a couple of bills
in the secret emergency compartment of her wallet. The
compartment was empty. Then she remembered she'd spent
it all when the girls went to the village to buy homecoming
gifts for their parents.

The waiter began to shuffle his feet restlessly. Angie
could feel her cheeks burning.

"What's the matter?" Gloria said, Edie's jacket tied at
her waist to cover the stain.

"Nothing . . . just a mix-up. About the tab. Some . . .
some mistake about my signature."

Edie looked at the bill, whistled softly.

Gloria took the bill from Edie, signed it. "No problem," she said to the waiter. Then to Angie: "Come on, let's get out of here."

When the parking valet brought up Gloria's Rabbit, she handed him a bill, slipped into the driver's seat. Angie plunged into the back, still smarting over the refusal of her signature. Angry and ashamed at once, she was close to tears.

Gloria drove the car down the tree-lined avenue to the exit gate, waited while the attendant opened it. She turned onto Sunset Boulevard, headed toward the freeway.

"Fasten your seat belts, folks," Edie joked. "Next stop, the slums, where the deer and the poor people play."

"I'm not going," Angie said in a small voice.

Edie turned and looked at her. "Hey, what's wrong with you? You're not upset over that stupid waiter, are you?" She laughed. "I've been refused credit all my life. You get used to it after awhile."

Gloria glanced into the rearview mirror, noticed Angie's pained reaction.

Edie went on babbling. "I'll never forget the time I had to wait at the credit office like some kind of criminal, while they checked my card . . . at Sears Roebuck's yet. I practically had to give them my finger prints and leave my fake fur jacket for security till they finally . . ."

"Take me home, Gloria," Angie said, her voice cracking unnaturally. "Please."

"But that's not the game plan," Edie protested. "We're going to my place, check out the guys on the beach. Gotta get there before all the other girls grab . . ."

"Shut up, Edie," Gloria said, as she made an abrupt right turn into a side street.

"But it's all arranged," Edie insisted.

"Edie, I can't . . ." Angie couldn't keep the urgency out of her voice, the pleading.

Edie opened her mouth for a comeback, but Gloria beat her to it.

"Keep quiet, Edie, okay?" Gloria said firmly.

"What'd I say?" Edie asked defensively. "Did I miss something or what? All I said was . . ."

Gloria shot her a fierce look and Edie clammed up. The car was headed back in the direction of Angie's house.

Angie sank deeper into the seat. She shouldn't have met the girls. She'd spoiled their day. She wanted to say she was sorry, but she knew if she opened her mouth she'd start crying.

The ride to Angie's house seemed endless. No one spoke, and they were all relieved when Gloria brought the car to a halt in the driveway.

Then suddenly, without willing it, Angie blurted out, "I'm not going back to Oakmont! I . . . I can't go back!"

The girls looked at her in open-mouthed surprise. Even Edie was too stunned to make a snappy retort. Finally, Edie say, "Why? Why can't you? Angie, what's going on?"

Angie shook her head, the tears brimming in her eyes. "I don't know. I don't know what's going on!"

Then she bolted out of the car and ran toward the house.

Chapter Seven

She didn't know how long she had been lying on her bed. Her eyes felt glued together with dried tears. She sat up slowly to see Nick standing in the doorway, looking at her intently.

"Go away," she said dully.

He stepped into the room and sat on a chair opposite her bed.

"Nick, please, I don't feel too good."

He looked at her coldly. "I've just been on the phone with Barbara Stender. And I've just been talking to Mother. Your mother and I don't see eye to eye on a certain proposition I put to her. I'm going to put it to you."

"Nick, I don't want to talk about anything right now."

"The proposition has to do with Barbara. Mother says I should call Barbara back and tell her not to come; to tell her we have illness in the family."

Angie didn't answer. She went to her bureau drawer for a clean handkerchief.

"I told your mother . . ."

Angie whirled around angrily. "Will you stop saying 'your mother'! You sound like second-rate movie dialogue, trying to be sophisticated."

"Angie, you're not too old to get a good clout in the face!"

"Just go away, Nick."

"Now you listen, because this proposition concerns you too. Barbara is coming in on American, Flight 47, Monday. I'm going to pick her up at the airport. When she gets here, it's going to look like this is a nice, normal, stinking rich but unpretentious Bel-Air family—Mommie, me, little sister. Everybody dressed just right, everybody saying just the right things, everybody making Barbara feel it wouldn't be too awful if these two families had a social connection. And maybe, who knows, a couple of years down the line—when Barbara and I get out of school—maybe the connection will be matrimonial."

Angie looked at him and shook her head sadly. She gestured out toward the pool and tennis court. "You really believe in all of this, don't you?"

"You bet your life I do."

"Get out of my room now, okay?"

Nick got up. "We're putting on an act, Angie, and you're going along. And if Dad gets back, he'll be going along. It won't be hard for him. He's used to being a phony."

Angie grabbed a metal bookend from the top of her bookcase and hurled it at him. It crashed into a picture on the wall. Nick smiled. Angie picked up the other bookend as Kathy came running down the hall.

Kathy stopped in the hallway. "Put that down, Angie."

Angie put down the bookend.

Nick turned to his mother. "I've just been giving her the scenario for Barbara's visit. She got a little violent."

"Mom," said Angie, "you're not going along with him?"

"Sure she is," Nick said.

Kathy looked at her two children. The fury between them filled the room.

"Nobody gets hurt," Nick went on. "We just put on a little show. It's a good investment for the future." He smiled at his mother. "Maybe 'investment' isn't the right word around here right now."

He stepped into the hall. "Tell her what you've decided, Mom." Then he went back to his own room.

Now Kathy saw Angie's red eyes. She went to her quickly, took her in her arms.

"Baby," she said softly, "it won't make any difference; it's just a little show."

Angie didn't move. Kathy held her closer. "Angie, baby, for all we know, it might not even be a show. Maybe Daddy will get it all together, after all."

Angie moved away, not looking at her mother. "Okay, Mom," she said dully. "It'll be okay."

"Look, Angie, when Dad comes home . . ."

"I said it's okay, Mom."

Kathy turned away. She looked at Angie's back, made a move toward her, stopped. She turned and left the room, shutting the door softly.

Angie went over to the picture she had smashed, picked it up off the floor. It was a Dufy print, a delightful watercolor of a day at the races; with prancing horses and gaily colored crowd. It had been a present from Ryan on her fifteenth birthday. A wonderful day.

It had been the end of summer, the last day before they were going back to their schools. They had planned to spend every minute of it together.

Night. The birthday dinner for two at Nan's hotel, the exclusive Bel-Haven. Nan was away and Ryan, as always, had the key to her rooms.

Angie knew he had the key, and he had said—trying to make it sound casual—"Maybe we'll have a nightcap in Nan's room, sit in front of the fire and just be alone."

Angie was startled by the suddenness of it. The big decision, the this-is-it dilemma. She could say no, it wouldn't look good, or maybe we should wait, or something. But this was Ryan. She loved Ryan. And she had to smile to herself at the way he put it. "Sit in front of the fire." In the middle of September? In the midst of a California heat wave, when the sundown temperature was a hundred and one? Oh, but she did love Ryan.

He looked across the table at her, smiling. "Another chocolate mousse?"

She laughed. "No way."

They were alone at a corner table. Nan's waiter had served them discreetly, giving them a sense of privacy. They weren't aware that other diners were looking at them wistfully, or with envious smiles.

"Happy birthday," Ryan said. He pulled a small package out of his coat pocket, set it in front of her. "I have another present, but this one is for now."

"Oh, Ryan . . ." she said. Then, looking down at the small package, "Can I guess what it is?"

"It's nothing. Just a little thing I picked up at Tiffany's. The salesman said it once belonged to an Indian maharajah."

She laughed and opened the package. It was a small silver ring with a turquoise stone set in a delicately carved mounting.

Angie took the ring out of the box.

"Actually," Ryan said, "I got it in New Mexico when I was a kid. I guess I must have been keeping it for you."

"It's lovely," she breathed.

"Hold out your third finger, left hand."

Angie held out the finger. The ring fit perfectly.

"Okay, now we're engaged. Tell your mother to send out the announcements."

Angie laughed. "Why not tell *your* mother?"

"That'd be the day," he said wryly.

She looked down at the ring, turning her hand slowly, letting the stone catch the candlelight.

"I'll bet you were a beautiful little boy in New Mexico."

"I was hideous. I had curls. I had to fight my way through every school I went to."

She looked at him tenderly. "Can we walk in the garden now?"

"If it's on the menu."

"It's supposed to come right after the dessert," she said.

He smiled, pushed back his chair. He had signed the check and left an elaborate tip for the waiter. They were bowed out with effusive smiles and soft thank you's.

The heat had died down a little; the night promised some coolness. They walked in the garden, then onto the footbridge above the small pond. Two white swans were resting near one bank, their heads hidden in their wings.

They stopped, leaned on the rail of the bridge. They were aware of the swans, the reflections in the water, the soft scent of nearby flowers. But most of all, they were aware of each other, shoulders touching, bodies alive to the promise of the night.

They stayed a long time on the small bridge; then, without saying anything, they moved hand in hand toward Nan's bungalow.

Ryan had seen all of this in fantasy. The two of them with a bottle of wine, sitting in front of the fire. The touch of hands and then, later, him saying—with a corny stage delivery—"Wouldn't you like to get into something comfortable?"

He laughed as he said the line to himself.

"What's funny?" Angie asked as he opened the door of the bungalow.

"Nothing," he said. "I was just thinking of an old movie."

Angie wasn't thinking of an old movie. She was thinking of Edie, and Edie saying, "It's no big deal, really, and if you honestly love the guy . . ."

"Hey!" Angie cried, startled. He had picked her up and was carrying her over the threshold.

"I saw this," he grunted, "in the same movie." He kicked the door shut with one foot. "Only I'll bet she didn't weigh as much as you do." He put her down. They looked at each other, ready to laugh. Instead, he put his arms around her and they kissed. When they finally moved apart, he tried to make it sound casual and worldly.

"How about a little fire?"

"A fire? Tonight?"

"Why not?" he said. He went over to the wall and pushed the air conditioner lever down to sixty degrees. "It's going to be chilly in here."

"Oh, Ryan," she said, suddenly serious. "I'm scared."

He smiled down at her. "Yeah, me too."

He opened the small refrigerator and brought out a bottle of wine.

She looked at the wine uneasily. She didn't much like the stuff. Mostly she just held the glass and pretended to be sipping so she'd look as if she was with it.

Ryan held up the bottle, read the label. "Chateau d'Yquem. Okay?"

"What is it?" Angie asked.

"French Grape-Ade."

He opened the bottle and poured the wine into two glasses on the coffee table in front of the fireplace. He pushed two chairs together behind the table, then bent down to light the gas stick in the fireplace. There were several fake logs on the andirons and one log of real wood on top. The small gas flame circled upward around the real log.

Ryan looked at Angie with a tender smile. "Come sit by the fire," he said as he handed her a glass of wine.

They sipped the wine and watched the gas flame singe the real log, letting it send the delicious smell of wood smoke into the room.

Ryan didn't know the next move. How long was he supposed to wait? Suddenly, he heard himself saying—in what he imagined to be a corny stage voice, but actually came out as a kind of croak—"Wouldn't you like to get into something comfortable?"

Angie looked startled. "I am comfortable," she said.

"I mean, wouldn't you . . ." He gestured vaguely toward the bedroom.

"Oh," Angie said.

"I mean, if you don't want to . . ." he added hastily.

She got up from the chair.

He looked up at her. "Angie, if you really don't want to . . ."

She kissed the top of his head and opened the bedroom door. She smiled back at him. "Three minutes," she said, and closed the door.

She touched the light switch. Soft lamps lit the bedroom.

And there was the bed standing right in front of her, like a large, quilted accusation. A surge of guilt, out of nowhere, engulfed her. Absurdly, she thought of her mother, of the little church they used to go to in the Valley, and of course, the seventh commandment.

Idiotic, ridiculous. This was Ryan, the one she loved. These weren't the old days; these were the eighties. When two people loved each other in the eighties, they loved, didn't they? So what was sex, after all?

She frowned. Well, what was it? She had given herself three minutes and she was going to find out.

Angie, come on, girl, stop shaking.

She sat on the bed and kicked off one shoe.

Then she slowly kicked off the other shoe.

Then she untied the sash around her skirt. Then she just sat there.

The door opened, and Ryan stood in the doorway.

"Turn out the light," Angie said softly.

Ryan turned out the light. The sitting room was already

dark, and through the door they could see the fireplace. The gas jet had been turned up and the real log was burning brightly.

"Close the door," she said.

Ryan closed the door. They found each other in the dark. They clung together. The kiss was fiery, devastating, revealing, endless.

Then Ryan took her hands from around his neck. Angie wished she could see his face, but it was too dark. Didn't he want her anymore? Was she doing something wrong?

She felt his hands fumbling with the buttons on her blouse, and she knew all was well. It was all going okay. The only thing was, he was having a bit of trouble with the tiny pearl buttons. Should she help him? Was that sort of thing done, or would it spoil the romance of it?

Angie sat there trying to decide what to do next. But the decision was made for her when she felt Ryan give up on the buttons and push her blouse up around her neck.

She would have liked to slip it off, but now the buttons were lost somewhere in the folds of the blouse and she couldn't get it up over her head.

She felt Ryan gently pull her down beside him on the bed. And she forgot all about the buttons, the blouse, whatever was supposed to happen next. All she knew was that she was beside him, loving him, kissing him. . . .

And then there was the most ghastly, weird beeping sound in the sitting room, like a hundred tortured rattlesnakes.

They both sat straight up.

"What is it? Ryan, what is it?"

"I don't know!" Ryan shouted over the noise. He got out of bed. "Turn on the lights . . . the lights!" he yelled as he tried to make for the door.

Angie felt around for the bedside lamp but couldn't find it. She heard a loud thump over the beeping and knew she had thrown the lamp onto the floor.

Then Ryan opened the door and a cloud of thick smoke nearly took his breath. He backed up, coughing, "The light, Angie, find the light!"

Angie rolled over to the other side of the bed and finally found the switch for the lamp on the nightstand. Her eyes were tearing, and she could hardly breathe.

Ryan ran to the window and threw it open. The smoke began to pour out of it. "Come on!" he yelled to Angie, "get out! Here, through the window!"

Angie ran to the window, sat on the sill. She was about to swing her legs over to the outside when she saw Ryan move toward the living room. "Ryan, come back, the place is on fire! Don't go . . ."

The beeping was threatening to burst her eardrums, but she heard Ryan yell, "The damper! I forgot to open the damper on the fireplace!"

Then she couldn't see him anymore. In a panic, she jumped to the ground, ran around to the front of the bungalow. There she was met by the hotel manager and the security guard tooling up on a luggage tram.

The security guard jumped off the tram, threw the door of the bungalow open, plunged into a cloud of smoke.

Angie heard Ryan coughing, the guard's voice yelling, "Turn it off! Turn the thing off!"

"What thing?" Ryan's voice sputtered.

"The smoke detector! Get out of here, I'll do it!" The guard stuck his head out the door. "No fire! It's only smoke!"

Ryan bolted out of the bungalow, nearly knocking Angie off her feet.

She recovered, only then realizing that her blouse was still twisted around her neck, the sash of her skirt dangling limply down her sides. She pulled her blouse down, looked at Ryan.

His face was blackened with smoke, his hair curled

damply around his face. His open shirt flapped outside his trousers.

By now, a couple of hotel employees were dragging a long hose to the door. Other guests from the nearby bungalows began to mill around.

"Get that hose out of here!" yelled the manager. "Nothing to worry about, folks," he said to the growing crowd. "There's no fire, just a smoke detector. No problem, folks, the heat triggered the detector accidentally."

The hose men retreated as the manager went from one guest to another, reassuring them, explaining about a freak accident . . . a defective smoke alarm.

At last, the security guard silenced the smoke detector and bolted out of the room, the smoke trailing after him.

Then the manager invited the onlookers to go to the bar and order anything they wanted—compliments of the house, of course. And that dispersed the crowd.

Angie and Ryan stood there while the manager went into the now smoke-cleared rooms to check them out. When he came out, Ryan smiled weakly and said, "I'm sorry."

The manager, who had known Ryan from the time he was eight years old and fell in the pond chasing the swans, returned the smile. "Did you really need a fire, Ryan?"

"Atmosphere," said Ryan, trying for a grin.

"Of course," the manager said. "Why don't you go in and get your things? The place will have to be guarded all night while it's being aired out."

Ryan brought Angie's shoes out, took her hand. "I guess we'll be going now," he said to the manager.

The manager gave Ryan a friendly tap on the shoulder, smiled at Angie.

As the two moved off, he shook his head and said softly to himself, "Atmosphere."

On the way home in Ryan's car, they didn't say much.

Angie put her head on his shoulder. He could feel her either crying or giggling.

"What's funny?" he asked.

"The whole thing," she said. "It all just seems so funny now."

And then they both began laughing together.

At last, Daddy was home from Texas, but it seemed incredible to Angie. Here they were, sitting around the breakfast table, the four of them, just like a normal family, Jim wolfing down the eggs and bacon, reading the financial section, Nick reading the sports page, Mom in the kitchen making another pot of coffee, and Angie pushing her cereal around in the bowl, absolutely dumbfounded that no one was saying a word, not one word about what had to be on everybody's mind.

Jim had arrived late the night before, to be greeted wildly by Angie, apprehensively by Nick and Kathy. Nobody asked the real questions. Just, how was the trip? How do you feel? Would you like a drink? Was it hot in Texas? Jim said he was dead tired and had to get to bed, but Angie could hear him and Mom talking for hours. And sometimes their voices had been raised higher than just plain conversation.

Nick seemed to be reading but he wasn't really. "What about Barbara Stender?" he asked out of nowhere.

Jim looked up from his paper. "Huh?"

"Barbara Stender. Mom says I ought to call her off, tell her not to come."

"Why?" Jim asked mildly.

Kathy was coming in with the coffee. "I'll tell you why," she said firmly. "Because we haven't got any help and I can't handle it alone."

"So get some help," Jim said.

"With what? Help won't take credit cards."

Jim smiled, picked up the coffee pot that she had set

next to him. "Now look, it's not that bad. I'll rustle up some help."

"Thanks, Dad," Nick said.

Jim picked up his cup, took a sip. "Hey, aren't we using that special Colombian coffee?"

"It's six dollars a pound," Kathy said. Then, "Jim . . ."

"Yeah?"

"It *is* that bad, isn't it?"

He looked at the three of them, smiled. "We're eating, aren't we?"

Kathy made an impatient gesture.

He looked around the breakfast room. "We've got a pretty nice house, haven't we?"

Kathy rolled her eyes ceilingward in exasperation.

"So Angie goes to public school for one semester. Is that so awful, Angie?"

Averting her eyes, Angie shook her head.

"And Nick'll have to play tennis on his own court. Right, Nick?"

Nick grinned. The Barbara Stender thing would be okay. "Right," he said.

"So we're really sitting pretty," Jim said looking up at Kathy. "All I have to do is go down to the bank and ask them to lend us a few dollars on the house."

Kathy was on the point of angry tears. "Jim, stop it! You're in trouble, we're broke! Let's quit playing games! Sell the house!"

"Sell the house!" Nick yelled. "What have we got if we lose the house?"

"We've got some self-respect!" Kathy yelled back. "All we lose is a false front, a showpiece, a business asset!"

"Hey, Kathy," Jim said softly. "Take it easy."

"That's all it is! An exhibit!" Kathy said loudly.

"I thought you liked your home," Jim said.

"I hate it! I've hated it from the first day." She gestured toward the living room. "All that icy cold furniture, those stupid pictures that Fran King put up there. I can't sit in the living room—it's like sitting in a decorator's showcase."

"So we'll change the decoration," Jim answered.

"With what?" Kathy exploded. "More credit cards? More unpaid bills, more headwaiters saying, "Sorry, ma'am, we can't accept your signature'?"

"Mom . . ." Angie broke in.

"Tell him," Kathy said to Angie. "Tell your father what happened at the Club."

"Mom, it wasn't anything, really."

"So who needs that Club anyway?" Nick said. "We'll join Pineview. That's got a lot more class."

"More class, more class," Kathy said vehemently. "We'll buy more class, so we can put on a bigger show." She looked down fiercely at Jim. "How do you like what you've done to your children?"

Jim looked at her impassively. "Kathy, take a half a Valium, you'll feel better."

Kathy looked at him in despair, turned, and left the room.

Jim looked sympathetically at Angie. "You didn't tell me about the Club."

"It's all right, Daddy."

"I'm going to call them," Jim said. "I'll talk to Jules. I won't have him treating you like that."

"Never mind, Daddy, it's all right, really it is."

Jim got up. "I'm going to talk to him anyway. Has your car got gas, Nick?"

"Yeah. What's the matter with yours?"

"Nothing. Steve Perry offered me a lot of money for it. I owed him a favor so I let him have it."

He kissed Angie on the cheek. "I'll take care of Jules. Don't worry."

Angie couldn't say anything more. With love and despair and a feeling of helplessness, she watched him leave the room.

Nick poured himself another cup of coffee, glanced at the financial section that Jim had left on the table. Idly, he turned a page.

Angie got up. She didn't feel like eating. Or being at the table with Nick.

"Oh, no . . ." Nick said softly. He looked up at Angie, who was halfway out of the room. "C'mere," he said.

She didn't move.

He gave her a cold look, then he read from the paper. " 'Careau Investments Under Investigation.' " He took a deep breath and continued: " 'The district attorney's office has revealed that James Careau will be questioned in a discovery hearing pertaining to allegations that Careau mismanaged large portfolios through unauthorized trading in commodity options. No details are available.' "

He crumpled the paper angrily, slammed it on the table. "That does it for Barbara Stender!"

Angie felt chilled, frozen. The newspaper words had hit her like direct blows, each one piercing, stabbing at her. She turned and ran down the hall, sobbing helplessly.

Chapter Eight

She threw the ball listlessly, and Duke shambled across the tennis court after it. Angie was sitting with her back wedged into a corner of the fencing, her knees drawn up, making herself small and inconspicuous. Unavailable. If someone phoned she couldn't be found. "Sorry, Angie isn't home. I think she's gone to Alaska or someplace. No, she went alone, just with her dog, Duke, and two large boxes filled with credit cards."

She sighed, looked around her. Everything was so complicated in Bel-Air. It had been nice and simple in the Valley. You knew who you were and where you were going. And you didn't have to buy fun; you made your own. And you felt like a family. You even did things with your folks.

Like that trip back to Iowa with Mom the summer Angie was twelve. That was the first time since she'd been married that Mom had felt she could afford the fare back home to visit her parents.

Nick was off to camp, so Angie got to go with Mom, a trip that, it turned out, had been nice but kind of weird in a way. Angie allowed herself an inward smile, thinking of her first cousin, Harold. Yeah, it had been kind of weird, all right.

*　　*　　*

"Well," Grandpa had said, looking down at her from his full six-feet-three, "she has your eyes, Kathy."

They had driven in Grandpa's pickup all morning from the airport at Des Moines, past endless fields of tall corn, and now they were in Regina, population thirty-five hundred, one main street, one Sears catalogue store, two farm implement stores, a post office, a general store, Hickman's garage, and, out at the edge of town, standing alone and austere, looking down Main Street with a watchful eye, was a very large, white church with a very tall steeple and a bell in the tower that could be heard for miles around.

But there were trees and cool, quiet streets with houses that had front lawns and porches. Grandpa's house even had a swing on the porch.

"Does she know her catechism?" asked Grandpa.

Mom evaded the question, and Angie didn't even know what a catechism was.

Grandma wasn't quite so awesome. She took her religion calmly. Grandpa had narrowly missed the ministry, having had to help on the farm during the Depression, but the church was his way of life.

Kathy had escaped from Grandpa's benign tyranny, but her older sister, Grace, who still lived in town, hadn't. Grace had married a tractor salesman, pinned him down to a house near Grandpa's, and they had produced one offspring, a boy named Harold.

And that was the weird part of Angie's two-week visit to her grandparents. Aunt Grace's boy, Harold. Angie's first cousin.

He was thirteen, one year older than she. He was overweight and had an odd smell, which wasn't exactly his fault but the result of feeding sour mash to his very intelligent pet pig.

They brought Harold over for Sunday dinner to meet his cousin Angie. He asked permission to give the blessing at dinner and got a nod of approval from Grandpa. Harold intoned the grace in an earnest imitation of his grandfather, but his piping voice didn't quite make it, and his eyes darted greedily around the food-laden table.

Angie, though only twelve, knew a weirdo when she saw one. She smothered a giggle and wondered how she could avoid him for two weeks. But Harold latched onto her, having no friends other than his intelligent pig.

Since play was not allowed on Sunday, they sat on the swing after dinner. They swung silently, Angie taking the far end of the swing. He kept looking at her very seriously.

Finally, he said, "Have you been redeemed?"

"What?"

"Do you accept our Lord Jesus as your Redeemer?"

Openmouthed, Angie looked at him.

"I do," he said.

"Well, that's nice."

They swung some more. Suddenly Harold said in a confidential tone, "I'm guilty."

"Huh?"

"Gluttony."

"Gluttony?" Angie repeated wonderingly.

He nodded sadly. "One of the seven cardinal sins. It's at the top of my list."

"What list?" Angie was beginning to feel stupid.

"My list of major spiritual defects." He brightened for a moment. "Prayer helps."

"Good," Angie said, not knowing what else to say.

"We're first cousins. I can tell you." Then in a strangled, choking voice, he told her all. He said that whenever he sinned in thought or deed, he refrained from eating sweets for all the days of his atonement. He said that abstinence from sweets was his "hair shirt," the way he punished himself for his weakness of the flesh. At the moment, he was in his eleventh day of repentance, and his craving for his favorite candy bar, a sinfully delicious sweet called *Plush*, was unbearable.

When he finished talking, Harold seemed much relieved. He leaned back and gave the swing some fresh momentum. "I'm glad I told you," he said.

Angie wasn't glad. She was embarrassed and bewildered and wished he'd go home.

There was a dull silence broken only by the creaking of the swing chains.

After a while Harold said, "Would you like to see Jedediah?"

"Who?"

"My pig, Jedediah." He smiled for the first time. "I call him Jed."

Angie thought of having a choking fit or maybe declaring she was coming down with the measles, but she was luckily saved by Aunt Grace and Uncle Fred, who took Harold off to the afternoon serices at the tall white church at the end of town.

But Harold pronounced as he left, "I'll be over to see you tomorrow."

And he was.

And the next day, and the day after that. On Monday, Angie met Jedediah, the pig. On Tuesday, her cousin took her window-shopping past the general store. Wednesday, Harold asked her formally for a date. And that night he took her to the Bible study class. On Thursday, he said, boldly, that she was the prettiest girl he had ever seen.

Harold was getting on her nerves. She hated to hurt his feelings, but she hated the way he smelled even more.

Something had to be done. She appealed to her mother.

"After all, he is your first cousin," Kathy said, repressing a smile.

"I know," Angie groaned.

"And he seems genuinely fond of you."

"Yeah. He told me he'd rather walk with me than Jed."

"Who's Jed?"

"His pig."

Kathy tried to hide it but she couldn't. She burst into laughter and hugged Angie. "Oh, Angie, Angie, it doesn't matter. It's just wonderful to have someone love you, isn't it?"

"Robert Redford would be better."

Kathy laughed again, holding her closer. "Robert Redford would never leave his wife, darling. Be nice to poor Harold."

"Okay," Angie sighed. "I'll be nice to Harold."

And she was. The next day she had a half-dollar in her pocket and she was determined to do something nice for Harold. So late in the afternoon, when they went to the general store so Harold could buy a packet of fifty assorted hand needles for his mother, Angie spotted a gooey marshmallow candy bar called *Plush* and bought it when he wasn't looking. She hid it in her sweater to surprise him on the way home.

The heat of the day had cooled, and they walked through the little park at the far end of town. Harold daringly suggested that they sit on a secluded bench hidden behind the trees near the small pond.

They sat on the bench. Harold's shoulder touched hers. He leaned closer.

Angie was overwhelmed by the strong smell of him. In quick defense, she took out the *Plush* bar and handed it to him.

"For me?" he asked, looking at the treasure sitting in his hand.

Angie nodded, moved to the edge of the bench.

He turned the bar over lovingly in his palm. "You bought this just for me?" he asked awesomely.

"No," Angie said. "I didn't buy it. I stole it."

"You what?" There was a stricken look on Harold's face.

Then the flash, the revelation, the ultimate solution hit Angie like a bomb.

"I stole it," she said calmly, "while you were buying the needles."

"You didn't!"

"I did. I just took it. Why pay when you can swipe?" Angie said airily.

"Stealing is a sin!" Harold said. "You broke the eighth commandment! You'll have to take it back!"

But Angie noticed that he didn't give the candy bar back to her.

"What's a little sin? Anyway, nobody saw me." She nodded at the bar. "Go ahead, open it."

"No!" But Harold clutched the bar.

"Mmm, it's delicious. Real marshmallow. With crunchy almonds."

"I can't! It's stolen!"

"Marshmallow and crunchy almonds with a creamy coat of chocolate," Angie teased. "Go ahead. It'll just melt in your mouth. You'll love it."

"The Book says, 'Thou shalt not steal,' " Harold said firmly.

"You didn't steal. I did."

"If I eat this I'm as guilty as you," he said, not so firmly.

"Okay." Angie held out her hand. "Give it back. I wouldn't want to lead you not into temptation." She hoped she had the quotation right.

Harold didn't hear her. Transfixed, almost in slow motion, he peeled the wrapper off the dark brown bar. He took a deep breath.

"Ohhh," Angie said. "Doesn't it look yummy?"

In one bite, Harold halved the bar. He chewed slowly, dreamily, blissfully.

Angie watched him in amazement. With no loss of jaw motion, he put the other half of the candy bar in his mouth. When, minutes later, he stopped chewing, he rose from the bench. It was as if he had awakened from a dream. His face was flushed; he looked anguished. "Now I'm as guilty as you are."

Angie nodded solemnly. "I guess we're just not good for each other, Harold."

"I guess not," he said gravely. "You're like . . . like Jezebel."

Angie, though only twelve, knew an exit line when she heard one. She touched him gently on the arm. "Goodbye, Harold."

Harold nodded, unable to speak.

"Give Jed a hug for me."

Sadly, Harold nodded again.

Angie ran out of the park and felt like laughing for joy all the way back to Grandpa's house.

But when she got there she had a terrible lump in her throat and felt like crying instead. She couldn't figure it out at all.

And she couldn't figure out who Jezebel was. It had to be someone in the Bible. She looked it up and spent the next week moping unhappily around the house.

Harold's mother couldn't understand why he absolutely refused to go over and play with his own first cousin.

But Kathy felt relieved when she finally got Angie back to California. And after that visit to Regina, Iowa, Angie didn't have to wonder why her mother always seemed so square.

Duke dropped the soggy ball at Angie's feet. She threw it again. Oh, to be twelve once more with such nice manageable problems. She sighed. If only Ryan were here. Not tomorrow, when he would be here, but right now, scrunched up beside her, holding her hand and telling her everything was going to work out. Which, of course, it wasn't. It really wasn't going to work out. How could it?

Daddy didn't get the loan at the bank, Barbara Stender

wasn't coming to Bel-Air, and even though it really didn't matter much, Jules, the headwaiter at the Club, had not been told off either. And the whole ghastly thing was out in the newspapers.

But that wasn't the awful, gut-wrenching, nerve-stretching part of it. The really awful part, the part she hadn't been able to see until it hit her right between the eyes in the newspaper: the dreadful possibility that her father, James Careau, the white knight riding, might well go to jail.

Jail. The slammer. Clang. The gates shut tight. Daddy grabs the bars, shakes them, yells to be let out. He calls her name. "Angie . . . Angie . . ."

She jumped up, her heart pounding.

"Angie!"

Jim had slid the living room door open and had been calling her. She pushed back against the fence as if to make herself smaller. She didn't want to talk to anyone right this minute, not even Daddy.

But Duke was at the gate of the court, wagging his tail, and she saw her father behind the wire of the fence. As she got up she had a horrible image of him behind the wire in the prisoners' visiting room, a picture she had seen many times on TV. It was awful.

"Hey!" Jim called out cheerily. "What are you doing there all alone?"

"Nothing," Angie said.

He opened the gate and gave her a hug. "I came home specially to find you," he said. "What day is today?"

"I don't know," she shrugged.

"It's my birthday, and we're going to take a ride to the beach. Just you and me."

"Your birthday is March twenty-fourth."

"Yeah, I know. But I've got to be in court on the twenty-fourth."

"Oh." Angie said. She looked up at him, understandingly. "Okay, what beach?"

"Malibu. Near the pier. And we'll eat lobster at the Fish Joint."

"Daddy . . ."

"Yeah?"

"Do you really think we ought to?"

He looked at her seriously. "Don't you?"

"I mean . . ."

"I know what you mean. The house is falling down; things are coming apart; the baddies are moving in."

"Aren't they?"

"Not yet, baby. I've got a little time. Anything can happen if you've got a little time."

He put his arm around her shoulder. "Should we take Duke?"

At the mention of his name, Duke wagged his tail.

"Mom says . . ." Angie began.

"I know. No dogs at the beach."

Angie smiled. "But Duke's not really a dog, right?"

"Right."

So they took Duke and got in the rented car that Jim was driving and went off to the beach.

Angie watched Jim, with Duke puffing at his side, jog along the edge of the water. He waved to her and she waved back. And she smiled to herself.

Only Daddy would think of this. With the world falling apart, his career rushing toward destruction, only he would scatter the demons with a day at the beach.

And what a day it had been. The first touch of spring had turned the brown hills behind them to vivid green. Small boats were sailing smartly in the March wind. The sand was warm; the air was cool.

They had lobster at the Fish Joint, and afterward they walked to a cove where the surfers were riding on high breakers that tossed them willfully on the beach.

Angie knew, behind all this wonderful day, there might

be some other use for the stolen time with daddy. In all the confusion and upset since she had been called back from Oakmont, there hadn't been a minute alone between them. No time to ask questions and get answers, just between the two of them.

He came back, puffing, dropped to the blanket beside her. Spraying wet sand on both of them, Duke shook himself.

Jim laughed, lay back in the sand with his hands clasped under his head, and looked up at the immensity of the blue sky above him.

"Angie . . ."

"Yeah?"

"Let's not ever go home. Let's be a couple of beach bums, okay?"

Angie smiled at him.

"We'll swim and surf and eat lobster twice a day. You and me and Duke. No problems. No obligations. Just three bums." He raised his head. "Okay?"

"Okay," she laughed.

He flopped back down again, looking once more into the infinity of blue. "No problems, no lawyers." He smiled wryly. "No money."

Angie waited.

"Angie?"

"Yeah?"

"What do you want to know?"

"Whatever you want to tell me."

He sat up slowly, brushed sand off his legs. "I didn't steal anything, Angie."

Angie nodded.

"Do you know anything about my business, baby?"

She thought. "You tell people how to invest their money, something like that."

"Yeah," he said. "Something like that. They give me a dollar and I give them back two dollars. And they say,

'Hey, Jim, that's terrific. How did you do it?' And I tell them I bought this pretty little stock and it doubled. And they say, 'Jimmy, boy, you're a wonder. Here's some more money. Do it again.' "

He picked up a handful of sand, watched it slide through his fingers. "I made a lot of money for a lot of people, Angie."

"I'll bet you did, Daddy."

"An awful lot of money." He sighed, looked off at the sailing boats. "Real big money." He looked at her now. "But it wasn't enough. I decided to make every client's dollar turn into three, not just two. So I took their money and gambled for them in the options market. For a while I was winning big and they were cheering me on. Then the market turned sour. I didn't get out fast enough; I was sure it would turn back. I lost a lot of money for a lot of people." He took a deep breath. "I wasn't Jimmy the wonder kid anymore. All of a sudden I was that crook, Jim Careau. A few of them got together and went to the district attorney and said I mismanaged their funds." He sighed. "Technically, I guess I did. I wasn't authorized to trade in options." He smiled. "If I'd won we'd be sitting on the sand in Bermuda or the Riviera right now."

"The sand's okay right here," Angie said.

"Yeah, it's nice sand." He looked at his watch, lay back on the blanket. "Why don't you and Duke go watch the surfers? I'll take five." He put his arm over his eyes, shutting out the sun.

Thinking hard, Angie walked slowly toward the edge of the water, trying to put it all in place. But it got jumbled. He gambled; he lost. He didn't steal; he mismanaged. It spun around in her head, not making too much sense. What was real? And what wasn't?

She stopped at the water's edge, looking back at him lying motionless on the blanket. She felt a sudden tenderness, an urge for some magic formula to make it all right, to put it back to where it had been this time last year when everything was solid, had meaning and direction.

She was suddenly reminded of her cousin Harold. How appalled he'd been when she told him she had stolen the candy bar. "You broke the eighth commandment," he had said. "Thou shalt not steal," he had said. But he had eaten the candy bar anyway.

Duke, yapping defensively, chased a wave and forced it to retreat. He looked up at Angie, offering to share the victory over the next one.

Angie smiled. "Go get it, Duke!"

Duke rushed the next one, and it hit him head-on and slapped him down ignominiously.

Angie laughed.

Duke shook himself and ran down the sand to show that he really wasn't serious about subduing waves; he was just kidding. Angie followed, running hard to keep up with him.

It had been a strange but beautiful day at the beach with her father.

Chapter Nine

Angie sat in front of her phone for hours waiting for the call from Ryan. She knew his plane got in at 9 A.M.; then it would be a half hour from the airport; then he'd have to visit with his parents. Say an hour for that. Of course, he could have called as soon as he got home, but maybe he'd have to fill his folks in about school and "back east" stuff.

Ryan went to a prep school in Connecticut in a town where some of his mother's family still lived. During school term he made duty calls on his aunts, knowing his mother would want all the news.

But he could have called as soon as he got home. He really should have. It was now almost noon. Of course, she could call him, but that might look funny. Or his mother might answer and that would be worse.

She tried willing the phone to ring, giving it sympathetic vibes, thinking of Ryan and feeling his wonderful closeness. She tried glaring at the phone, walking away from it. Phones usually rang when you ignored them, but she wasn't truly ignoring it. And she only got as far as the end of the hall and the entrance to the living room when she heard the frontdoor chime.

She ran to the door and flung it open.

"Ryan!"

He stood there with a half-smile, but not holding out his arms. So Angie threw her arms around him and held him tight, and moved her face back for a kiss.

He kissed her, but not in the way she had imagined he would. Not with the wild, us-against-the-world-hold-me-forever embrace she had projected onto the screen in her head every day since she had come home.

He held her at arm's length, looking at her intently.

She was startled, unprepared. "Well, hello," she said feebly. "Welcome home."

"Hello," he said. "Let's go sit by the pool."

He moved away from her, crossed the living room quickly. Outside Duke jumped up and greeted him. He patted the dog absently, then flopped onto a deck chair.

Angie stood at the sliding glass door of the living room. He motioned for her to come and sit at the end of the chaise. She crossed the flagstoned deck slowly and sat down.

"I just had a big hassle with my folks," he said.

Angie breathed a sigh of relief. That explained it. "Oh, Ryan, I'm sorry."

"About what?"

"Nothing. I'm just sorry you had a big hassle."

"It was about you."

She looked at him anxiously.

"Well, maybe not you, maybe your father." He made an impatient, angry gesture. "I don't know, the whole thing was stupid. I told them, 'I'm going with Angie, not her father. What's her father got to do with anything!' "

He scowled at Angie. "It's us, isn't it? No matter what he's done, it'll always . . ."

He broke off, seeing Angie's stricken look.

Angie's heart pounded in undefinable fear. "What else did you say?"

"Nothing," he said softly. "You know my mother."

Angie nodded miserably.

"Angie . . ." He took her in his arms and stroked her hair gently. "I'm sorry, Angie."

She leaned against him, not talking.

"Angie, I've missed you."

She mumbled something against his chest.

"I've been figuring out all the things we were going to do on this vacation." he said. "We're not going to do them, are we?"

She sat up, shook her head, not able to speak.

"When are you going back to school?" he asked.

She took a deep breath. "I'm not going back."

"Huh?"

"I'm not going back." She turned her head away, looking at Duke. "There isn't any money."

"Oh."

"Nick isn't going back to USC, either."

"Oh," Ryan said again.

"What did your mother say? In the hassle?"

"A lot of junk."

"Like?"

"Like why don't I go down to the Springs for this vacation, do something different."

"Why don't you?"

"Do you want me to?"

"No. But she does."

"Okay, but that's not me."

"What's you?"

He looked at her tenderly. "Angie . . . Angie . . . are we going to fight?"

"Maybe."

"No, we're not," he said. "C'mere."

She looked away from him. Why hadn't he just told his mother off, told her that nothing mattered but the two of them? Why hadn't he stormed out of the house and let them know he was running his own life? Why did he just say . . . nothing?

"C'mere, Angie."

She got up. "I've got to feed Duke."

He laughed, jumped up, grabbed her. "He's not hungry."

"Let go, Ryan."

He turned her face around, kissed her just the way he should have in the first place.

When he let her go he took her hand, and then started to embrace her again.

She stopped him gently. "My mother's home."

"Oh," he said with a smile. "I thought she went to the hairdresser on Wednesday."

"She doesn't go to the hairdresser anymore."

He took his arm from around her waist. "Okay, we can wait. Let's feed Duke."

At first, Angie was going to skip the big party at Gloria's house; she simply didn't have the heart for it. But Gloria had been pathetically insistent. How could she possibly bring off a party without Angie?

At all of Gloria's past parties, the three girls fell naturally into their respective roles. Gloria, the official greeter, looking beautiful, being gracious, met the guests at the door. Edie, the conversationalist, kept the gang laughing at her jokes, her witty remarks. And Angie, the manager, the stage director, broke up cliques, kept the crowd mingling.

Having observed Fran King so many times, Angie had developed a real talent for keeping the festivities at just the right level. She had a good sense of timing. She knew when the music needed to be blasting; she knew when to tone it down. She knew when the food ought to be served, and she sensed—instinctively—when the party might get out of hand, the exact time to call it a night. Usually, that was when couples wandered off, hand-in-hand, to secluded nooks and crannies or when the odor of something stronger than tobacco began to be noticed.

But always, Gloria's parties were the most fun. And

Gloria—with the help of her two best friends—was considered to be the very best of hostesses.

Angie had tried to tell Gloria she couldn't make it to the party, but Gloria had pleaded with her. "You've got to come. I'm counting on you. Please, Angie, if you don't come, I'll just have to call it off."

So Angie was there early, checking on the food, choosing the cassettes, calming Gloria's pre-party anxieties.

When everything was ready, Angie went into Gloria's room to freshen up. She sat down before the mirror, drew her comb through her hair.

She'd be glad when the party was over. At least if Ryan were coming there would be some chance of her having a good time. But Ryan's dad had been called out of town, and Ryan was escorting his mother to the Music Center for a concert. Angie really felt like going home right then, but she couldn't let Gloria down.

The bedroom door opened and Ellen, one of the new girls at Oakmont, stood there, looking surprised. "Oh, I didn't know . . . I mean, I didn't think you'd be here."

Angie recognized her. "It's okay, come in. Throw your jacket on the bed."

Ellen hesitated, then came into the room, looked past Angie's shoulder into the mirror. Ellen was a tall, thin girl, rather plain-looking. Word had it that her family was in oil, had homes in Oklahoma, Hawaii, Nice, Switzerland. She grinned at Angie's reflection. "I'm just so excited, I can hardly stand it!" she gushed.

Angie smiled. "You'll have fun, don't worry."

Ellen laughed nervously. "You don't know what this means to me . . . being invited. My being new and all."

"You'll be fine; you'll see."

Ellen went to the bed, put her jacket on it, sat down. "Oh, it's not just the party. I mean the party's great, but all the rest . . ."

Angie turned and looked at Ellen. "The rest?"

"Taking your place and all! Imagine me, only just enrolled, and already sharing a room with Gloria and Edie! I mean, I could die!"

Angie stared at her.

"I mean, the first day I came to Oakmont, I knew the three of you *were* the school. Then, when Edie called last night and offered your place to me . . ."

"My place?"

"In the dorm . . . your room. I suppose you're going to school in Europe or something, but I'm glad . . . I mean, wow, me in your room!"

Angie felt suddenly cold. "Edie called you?"

"Last night, like I said. And she's coming to Hawaii with me next summer. She said . . ."

Edie opened the door, stepped into the room. "Better come down, Angie. Gloria's got her parents' big band music mixed up with the rock and . . ." She noticed Ellen. "Oh, hi, Ellen."

"Hi, Edie," Ellen said cheerily.

Angie stood up, white-faced, trembling with anger.

Edie looked at Angie, then back at Ellen. "Go down and help Gloria. Okay, Ellen?"

"Sure thing," Ellen said eagerly, and left the room quickly.

"What'd she tell you?" Edie asked cautiously.

"Angie's out; Ellen's in."

"Come on, Angie, what difference does it—"

Angie interrupted. "Was Gloria in on it too?"

"I haven't had a chance to tell her yet. But, look, Angie, what did you expect?"

"A little . . ." She groped for the word. "A little decency. The body's hardly cold."

Edie spoke sharply. "Come off it, Angie, someone had to replace you."

"You don't even *like* the girl. 'Ellen, gushing like her father's oil wells.' Isn't that how you put it?"

"All right," Edie said. "So money matters to me. It matters to everyone who hasn't got it. You'll find out. You'll find out, now that you haven't got any."

Angie shook her head. She couldn't take it in. This was her friend Edie talking. Her friend!

Edie went on: "Wake up, Angie. It's a buy and sell world. I took you through Latin; you took me through the Country Club. That's what it's all about. Give and take."

Suddenly, Angie's anger was gone. Where the rage had been was only an emptiness, a hollow void. She sat down, her shoulders slumping forward.

She spoke softly, more to herself than to Edie. "I thought it was all about something else. I thought it was all about loyal friends."

Nan had arranged the luncheon for Angie and Ryan on the patio of her bungalow. The setting was springtime itself, the narrow border of the patio bright with flowers, the miniature orange tree in its redwood tub filling the small area with the fragrant scent of its tiny white blossoms. Sunlight sprinkled onto the umbrella table through the lush foliage surrounding the little terrace.

Angie pretended to listen to Nan's plans for her usual summer jaunt to Europe. But Angie wasn't really hearing her.

Ryan had called this morning to say he'd pick her up at eleven-thirty. "We promised Nan we'd be there, remember?"

Angie hadn't remembered. She'd forgotten all about it. So much had happened since she and Ryan had made the date with Nan only about a week ago. "I'm really not feeling too well, Ryan," Angie had said. "Maybe you'd better go by yourself."

There had been no answer for a moment, and it flashed through Angie's mind that perhaps Ryan would just as soon go alone. Then he said, "Nan would be disappointed.

We'd better go." But he hadn't sounded very enthusiastic. And on the short drive to the hotel, the two of them had hardly spoken. Despite the bright sunshine, the sparkling clear day, there seemed to be a pall—like a thick brown smog—hanging over them.

Nan put down her coffee cup. ". . . then after we pick up the bag I left at the luggage repair shop, we could take in a movie at the *Century*." She looked at Angie. "That is, if it's all right with you, my dear."

Angie was listlessly pushing her salad around on her plate.

"If you don't care for the chicken salad, we can order something else," Nan said. "Angela? Angela?"

"What?"

Nan looked closely at Angie, then at Ryan. "It wasn't important," Nan said. She poured coffee into Angie's cup. "We don't have to go to the movies."

"The movie sounds fine," Ryan said dully. He looked over at Angie, and she knew he was signaling her to agree.

Angie nodded. "Okay," she said.

And then there was silence, and all that could be heard was the chirping of birds and the far-off, ugly buzz of a gardener's leaf blower. Angie watched a hummingbird hover over the orange blossoms.

The parakeet. Angie hadn't thought about her pet bird in years. She had called him Blue. At the age of seven, it seemed the perfect name for him from the moment she'd seen him in the pet store window. And she had saved her allowance for six weeks that summer to buy him.

He was so beautiful, deep royal blue with a milk-white head and black spots around the top of his breast. And his wings were mottled, black-and-white, looking almost striped.

When Angie brought the bird home, Mom had declared that Angie would be the one to take care of him, clean his cage, feed him. She would have the total responsibility for her pet.

And Angie had cared for Blue with love and diligence. She kept his cage sweet-smelling, changed the paper every day. She even hung the cage on a branch of the apricot tree in the yard to air him when the weather wasn't too hot.

Then one sunny day, when she went out into the yard to bring him back in, she had found the cage door open and Blue lying lifeless at the bottom.

She knew, instantly, who had killed him. It was that mangy cat that had jumped the fence time and again to sit under the tree, its hungry eyes on the bird. Many times, she had chased the cat off; once she had hosed him down. But he had kept coming back.

Angie had been heartbroken. And guilty. If she had locked the cage door properly; if she had remembered to tie up the faulty door; if she had guarded her pet against the cat.

After she had buried him that day, she couldn't understand why the sun was still bright, why the kids on the block were still playing, laughing. How could the world go on as if nothing had happened? As if there had never been a beautiful bird called Blue. Angie had been angry. She had been angry with the sun, the kids, the world.

Nan broke the silence. "Wouldn't it be nice," she mused, "if the two of you could come with me?"

Angie wrenched herself back to the luncheon table.

Ryan said, "We *are* going with you, Nan. The luggage place, then the . . ."

"No, I mean to Europe."

"Oh, sure," Ryan said, dismissing the idea with a wry laugh.

"Why not?" Nan persisted. "What a wonderful time we'd have!"

Ryan smiled. "You've gotta be kidding. We could never get Mother to agree."

"Of course we could," Nan said. Then to Angie, "I'll talk to your parents. Give them our exact itinerary . . ."

"I couldn't," Angie said. "there's no money for . . ."

"Angela, dear," Nan broke in. "What else have I to do with my money? And how could you refuse an old lady a pleasurable summer?"

"You do mean it!" Ryan said. "Hey, Angie, it's some idea!"

Angie shook her head. Nan was precious; she meant well. But Angie couldn't accept such an extravagant gift. And, more important, no way would she leave Dad, the way things were.

"Think about it," Nan said. "Both of you."

Ryan and Angie looked at each other. From the expression on his face, Angie knew Ryan was all for the idea.

A summer with Ryan! A whole romantic, beautiful summer in Europe with Ryan! Of course, it was impossible, but for a moment she let herself drift with the notion. She and Ryan strolling through the streets in Paris, gliding on the canals in Venice, motoring over the mountains in Switzerland . . .

There was a knock on the door. "That must be the waiter," Nan said. "Let's have a terribly fattening, unhealthy, delicious dessert."

Nan crossed the living room, opened the door.

It wasn't the waiter. It was Ryan's mother.

Evelyn followed Nan to the patio. "There was a marvelous sale at Bonwit Teller. I picked up some of those hand towels you've been wanting . . ." She stopped when she saw Ryan and Angie, her face expressionless.

"Sit down, Evelyn. We were just having lunch. Coffee?" Nan said pleasantly.

Ryan stood up. "Hello, Mother."

Evelyn looked past him, her eyes on Angie.

"Ryan?" she said questioningly.

Ryan flushed uncomfortably but said nothing.

Angie wondered if his mother had asked him not to see her anymore. When they'd had that first encounter, had Ryan's mother told him to stay away from her? Angie waited for him to say, "Mother, you can't keep Angie and me apart. We love each other. There's nothing you can do about it."

But Ryan said nothing. Looking guilty, he sat down.

Nan swept her eyes over all of them, then said quietly, "I'm glad you dropped in, Evelyn. I was just telling Ryan and Angela I'd like to take them with me when I go abroad this summer."

Evelyn stood rigidly at the French doors to the patio. "Don't be ridiculous, Mother." Then to Ryan: "I'm truly disappointed in you, Ryan. We did have an understanding. It's obvious you didn't tell your grandmother . . . or your little friend."

"For heaven's sake," Nan said to Evelyn. "You sound like something out of a Victorian novel." She laughed tightly, trying for lightness. "Now sit down and have some coffee with us."

Evelyn pinned Nan down with steely eyes. "Mother, I'll thank you to stay out of our business. Ryan is my son; I know what's best for him." She looked pointedly at Ryan. "It is not in his best interest to go traipsing through Europe with a foolish old woman and a girl."

Nan's face paled. She started to speak, then looked at Ryan.

Angie held her breath. Ryan, Ryan, say something! Do something! Tell her what you've told me! Tell her, it's me and Angie; that's all that matters! Tell her, Ryan!

A bit softer now, Evelyn said, "Ryan, it's not like you to go back on your word."

Ryan looked down, his face red. He squirmed in his chair. "I'm . . . I'm sorry, Mother."

Evelyn turned, made for the front door. Over her shoulder, she said, ''I'll expect you home in an hour, Ryan.''

Angie kept staring at him. Finally, she turned her face away.

She could hear only the twitter of birds and the rasping buzz of the gardener's leaf blower.

Chapter Ten

Angie was trying to read but it was no use. The fast-moving plot of the detective story kept eluding her. She turned back to re-read pages, but the names got jumbled, and Ryan, Nan, and Ryan's mother moved in and out with the people in the mystery.

She had closed the door of her room, signaling the need for privacy. The clock on her desk said eleven-thirty; it was time for bed. She shrugged. Why bother? Why get undressed, brush teeth, sleep, get up? Why get up? What's to get up for?

Sleep. Now that was something else. If she could go to sleep and never get up. Come off it, Angie. Melodramatic. Hamlet stuff. But the idea did have some merit. Not to have to remember how happy she had been with Ryan . . . the promise of their relationship. And how dismally it had all ended. How disappointing. How painful.

But maybe, just maybe, it wasn't all over. Even now Ryan could be telling his mother off. She'd surprised him at Nan's place. She'd caught him off guard. He hadn't wanted to have a hassle in front of Angie and Nan. Once he got home, he'd have told his mother what he had told Angie over and over. "It's Angie and me . . . that's all that matters."

But way down deep . . . deep inside her, Angie knew she was lying to herself. Or was she?

Come on, Angie, find out why the wealthy Mrs. Harrington was found dead, face-down on the living room floor of her penthouse apartment on Sutton Place. Hey, wait, maybe that was a clue, *face-down*. If she had been strangled as Detective Garrity suspected . . .

Nick stood in the doorway of her room. She sat up, startled.

"Don't you ever knock?" she said.

He smiled, knocked on the doorjamb. He came in, plopped on the big chair. "What are you reading?" he asked.

Angie held up the book.

"I read it," he said. "Her nephew did it."

"Thanks."

He smiled some more. She was always very wary of Nick when he smiled.

"Her nephew was on dope," Nick said. "Cocaine."

Angie put the book down. "Good. Now, I don't have to read it."

"It's a lousy story anyway. I figured it out at about page thirty." He looked at her, still smiling. "Hey, Angie?"

"Yes?"

"How're you fixed for money?"

Oh, that was it. Aloud she said, "What do you mean, how am I fixed?"

"I mean, how much have you got in your savings account? Could you write a check for two hundred?"

"I've never written a check on that account."

"You got a checkbook same time I did."

"So write your own check."

"All right, don't be wise. I wouldn't be asking you if I could write my own. Can you let me have two hundred?"

"Why?"

"Why?" He looked up at the ceiling. "Because I need

two hundred, and you've got two hundred and thirty in your account."

"How do *you* know?"

"I looked this afternoon." He leaned over the desk, opened the top drawer, and tossed out her checkbook.

"Nick, I'd like to go to bed, so go away, will you?"

"You want to know why I need two hundred?"

"No."

"Okay, I'll tell you. I've got a standing invitation to go to Scottsdale, Arizona, and spend a couple of weeks with a guy I know at school. I called and told him I was coming. His family is loaded. All I need is money to get there."

"You can't go to Scottsdale," Angie said. "You have to be here on the twenty-fourth."

"For what?"

"Daddy's going to court."

"So?"

"So you heard what the lawyer said. It always looks better if the family is there."

"So you and Mom'll be there."

"Nick, the lawyer said it's terribly important."

"What's all this family crap? The judge'll ask him how he pleads. 'How do you plead, bub, guilty or not guilty?' Does the judge care if his family is there?"

"It's not just the judge," Angie said earnestly. "It's the whole"—she searched for the word—"the whole atmosphere. If his family believes in him . . ."

"You believe in him?"

"Yes. Yes, I do."

"Okay, so you go to court."

"Nick, please don't go away right now. He needs us, all of us."

Nick laughed, raised his eyes heavenward. "Angie, that's a lot of bull." Then he scowled. "He never needed me. You, okay. Not me."

"That's not true."

"Okay, okay, it's not true. Deep down he really loves me. Angie, write out a check for two hundred, will you?"

"Nick, he does love you."

"Good. Peachy. I love him." He held out his pen.

"I'm not going to help you walk out on him."

He looked at her angrily. "I'm going anyway."

"Please, Nick."

"And I'll let you in on a little secret. I might not come back. Ever."

Pleading silently, she looked at him.

"I can get a job at the tennis club out there. I'm good enough to teach kids, anyway."

"Go after the day at court."

He shook his head. "I'm going now. Tonight. I want to cross the desert while it's cool." He looked at her a long time, then suddenly seemed to lose all will to fight. "Aw, Angie, this is a losing game here. I can't take it. I really can't. I've got to get out. I can't help him and he can't help me. I've got to go."

Angie picked up the checkbook, took his pen. She wrote the date, looked up at him. "You're not coming back?"

"Not if I can hack it out there."

"Have you told Mom?"

He shook his head. "Nobody. Just you."

Angie wrote out the check, tore it off and handed it to him.

"Thanks, Angie," he said.

"Don't go, Nick."

"I have to."

They looked at each other a moment, all the stress and anxiety and pain suspended. He put the check in his shirt pocket. "You're a good kid, Angie," he said. Then he went to the door and closed it softly behind him.

She sat by the window, looking out at the pool for a long time. Then she turned out the light and lay on the bed, not bothering to get undressed.

Soon she heard Nick's car back out of the garage, turn, and go down the hill. She didn't think she could ever cry over her brother. But she was certainly crying about something.

Angie didn't tell her father that Nick wasn't coming back. Jim didn't admit that he wanted his son to be with him the day he went to court. But Angie knew he did.

Jim didn't admit that he wanted all of them to be there to hear him plead not guilty, and that he wanted to have them at his side as he left the court to face possible flashbulbs and questions from the press. But Angie knew he wanted that too.

Not guilty? Of course, not guilty. That was something else Angie knew. Hadn't her father explained it all that day on the beach?

He had gambled and lost, but he didn't steal. They couldn't pin that on him, his lawyers said. Sure, he mismanaged client funds. So what they *could* pin on him was three to five years and a whopping fine. Jim had laughed at that. What would they take for money? A credit card?

But there was one outside chance, the lawyers had said. One way he might squeeze out of it. If he could raise forty or fifty thousand dollars, and promise restitution of the rest, he might escape jail. The court could put him on probation till he earned back the money and paid everybody off.

And Angie knew her father would somehow raise the money. He had to. He just had to.

They were having supper in the kitchen. Hamburgers and fries. Angie had done the dinner.

"It's worth taking a chance, anyway," Daddy said.

"What?" Mom asked, looking up from her plate.

"Haven't you been listening?" he asked mildly.

"About what?"

He sighed. "The party. It might just be worth taking a chance and giving the party."

"What party?"

Angie couldn't stand this witless exchange. "Daddy wants to give a party for his business friends."

Mom looked at Daddy in bewilderment. "Why on earth would you want to give a party at a time like this? You mean a party here, at this house?"

"Of course, at this house." He pulled a piece of paper out of his shirt pocket. His voice was earnest, excited. "Listen, Kathy, these are guys I made a lot of money for. They got out before the trouble. I've been keeping in touch. I think they've still got confidence in me. If I could hit a couple of them for twenty, thirty thousand . . ."

"You're out of your mind, Jim."

He sighed, put the paper back in his pocket. "I figured you'd say that."

"But it's absurd."

"No." He shook his head. "Not absurd. I'm going to do it."

"You can't."

He turned to Angie. "Get me a little more coffee, will you, baby?"

Angie got up, looked at her mother and father uneasily.

"Jim . . ." Kathy began.

"Listen, honey, these guys are loaded; they're party hounds. They love the booze and excitement. Twenty thousand, thirty thousand is nothing to any one of them. If I put together a little holding company . . ."

"Jim, I will not give that party."

"Sorry," Jim said quietly. "I will."

"You'll have to find some other hostess."

"I'll do that too."

"Maybe you could get Fran King," Mom said tartly.

"Maybe I could. Maybe I will."

Angie looked from her mother to her father. There

was a determined, set look on Jim's face. Angie felt frightened.

"Jim, can't you see what you're doing?"

"Sure, I see. I'm taking a long shot. Maybe it works, maybe it doesn't."

Mom shook her head. "No, no, it isn't that. It's the whole idea. Using your house, your family to put on the same old show, pretending you're not in trouble."

"Kathy, you owe me this chance."

"Why?"

He looked at her pleadingly, started to say something, but she went on: "Why do we go on propping up this false front?"

Angie's hand trembled as she poured coffee into her dad's cup. Some of it spilled onto the counter. She reached over the sink for the sponge, mopped up, and picked up the cup.

"Would you rather call the whole thing quits?" Dad said.

"Yes."

Angie turned and stared at them. Her father forced a smile. "All right, honey. Maybe you need a vacation. Go back and visit your folks. I'll handle the party."

Mom took a deep breath. "I want a divorce, Jim."

Angie dropped the coffee cup in the sink. It broke in a hundred little bits. They didn't even hear it.

Daddy looked at Mom in total disbelief. "Kathy . . ." he began.

"I want a divorce," she said tightly. "I've already talked to a lawyer."

"Kathy, Kathy . . ." He shook his head slowly. "That doesn't make sense. You and I . . ."

"Not you and I anymore." She gestured toward the living room. "I don't want any more of this, Jim. No more of this life-style, no more fun in the fast lane." She got up from the table.

"Sit down, honey. Let's talk."

"We have talked. Endlessly. You just haven't listened."

"Kathy, a little vacation . . . maybe the two of us . . ."

She shook her head.

Angie was frozen to her place at the sink. With pounding heart, she watched the two of them. She hoped her father would say the right thing, pull out his old magic, make her mother take back those awful words. But her mother looked at her father and said the words again.

"I'm getting a divorce, Jim." She went to the door of the kitchen, stopped. She looked back at him despairingly. "I love you, but I'm not going to live with you anymore. I just can't."

She left the kitchen quickly.

Dad looked at Angie, still anchored to the kitchen counter.

"She didn't mean it, Daddy."

He got up, took out another coffee cup, and moved slowly, numbly to the counter.

"She really didn't mean it. I know she didn't."

He held out the cup; Angie poured the coffee.

"She meant it," he said.

"But she said . . ."

"Yeah," he answered dully. "She loves me; I love her." He took a long swallow of the coffee, put down the cup.

He went down to the end of the counter, picked up the phone. "I guess I'll have to get Fran King to run the party."

Chapter Eleven

It wasn't easy for Angie to deal with it. Even though half the girls in her class lived with divorced parents, Angie never thought it would happen to her.

Neither did Daddy. For once his boundless energy seemed to flag. He sat long hours in the kitchen downing endless bottles of beer and phoning Mom.

Numbed by mountains of futile talk, Kathy had fled to her friend Marge Keller's house for a few days. She said she'd be back after the party. Then when Jim's troubles were settled, one way or another, there would be time to make plans about the divorce.

The party now seemed to Angie like an approaching nightmare, like the evil climax of all that had gone wrong since she had come back from Oakmont. It couldn't have been only a few weeks since then, but it was. Everything had fallen apart quickly. A month ago she had been looking forward to spring vacation, to parties, friends, Ryan. Now, nothing but this ghastly party, this last desperate gamble. And after that? Zero. Zilch. Nothing at the end of the tunnel.

Angie went through her closet. She didn't have many dresses. The emerald green would have to do. She remembered briefly the excitement of buying the dress with Gloria last Christmas. She saw herself in the mirror at

Magnin's, the promise of the dress, the daring low cut, the slinky look of the long, tapered sleeves. She saw herself with Ryan and Nan at the Bel-Haven for dinner, the triumph of the dress, the perfection of the evening.

Listlessly, she dropped the dress on the bed. All that could have been a hundred years ago.

She looked at the clock. The party was to begin about eight. The caterer's truck had already arrived and the table was being arranged in the dining room. An extra bar was being set up in the library.

Dad was nervous, excited, like a race horse at the gate. He came in to check Angie's dress, thought it was too sophisticated, then wondered aloud if she ought to go to a movie instead of the party. When Angie said okay to the movie, he immediately said, no, he needed her. There had to be someone in the family present. It had to look right.

When he left her room, Angie plopped in her chair, wishing it were all over. From her window, she saw Fran King arrive.

Deftly, Fran took over as if it were her own home, which, in a way, it was. It was her creation, authenticated by a series of stunning photographs in *Decorative Arts Magazine*. Angie remembered the pages, the captions: "Residence of Mr. and Mrs. James Careau, Bel-Air, California. Architect, Joan Fenner; Interior Decorator, Frances King." What a day that had been, when the posh, ten-dollars-a-copy magazine came out with pictures featuring their home. "We're in!" Dad had yelled. "We made it!"

There was a discreet tap on the door, and Fran came in as Angie, adjusting the dress, stood in front of the mirror.

"It's lovely," Fran exclaimed. "You look like a young Natalie; the way she looked twenty years ago."

Fran had the peculiar habit of dropping first names. The persons on whom the name was dropped had to guess whom Fran was talking about. Usually, it was someone in films. Angie didn't bother to guess.

Looking in the mirror, Fran stood behind Angie.

"Is your young man coming? Ryan, isn't it?"

"No," Angie said. "He's not coming."

"Well, I don't think you'll lack company, dear."

Angie tried to smile but didn't quite manage.

"Of course, they'll be mostly older men, friends of your father's. You've met Don Nagle, haven't you?"

"Yes. He's repulsive."

Fran laughed. "Yes. He is."

"He paws."

"Yes, he does."

"He was one of Daddy's first clients. I always try to be somewhere else when he comes to visit."

Fran smiled, avoiding comment. She touched Angie's cheek. "A little eye shadow maybe?"

"I don't use it," Angie said, a touch tartly. Then, quickly sorry, she added, "Actually, I'm not very good at it."

"Want to learn?"

"I guess so."

Fran extracted a small box of eye make-up from her evening bag. In minutes, Angie's eyes grew larger and more interesting. She not only does houses, Angie thought, she does people.

When Fran left, Angie looked in the full-length mirror at someone she hardly recognized. For a moment she forgot the party and enjoyed the fun of being someone else, maybe that long-ago Natalie whose name Fran had dropped.

Angie heard the faint sound of music coming from the living room. She went to the back window of her room. The first car was pulling into the driveway, and the boy from the valet parking service was opening the door. The car, predictably, was a white Rolls, and the guest, predictably, was on the way to being drunk. He stumbled out of his car and walked unsteadily toward the entrance of the house. The party had begun.

Playing records and watching the cars arrive, Angie waited in her room as long as she could. Checking the green dress, she went to the mirror a dozen times. She scowled at her reflection each time, added a string of beads to the costume, took off the beads on the next trip, erased some of Fran's make-up, smeared it, put it back on.

Almost an hour later, Jim rapped on the door and came in. "Hey, honey, the party's waiting for you. Come along!"

Jim, high on pure energy, was wisely laying off the booze. The party was going well; the right people were there; the big money was walking the social jungle, all unaware that it was being deftly snared in Jim's charming net.

Angie was swept out into the party, introduced, flattered outragously by the men, observed shrewdly by the wives and girl friends, fussed over. "So lovely, charming, so unpretentious."

She smiled her way through it, passing from group to group as each acknowledged her, going along with the bright chatter that passed for conversation.

There was high alcoholic laughter, much serious discussion of films, of the stock market, of the idiots in Washington, quiet in-the-corner talk of who was sleeping with whom, and why, and, in lowered voices, why wasn't *she* there? Kathy, his wife.

Angie got out of it by offering to refill drinks. She watched her father talking easily with several men who seemed to be nodding their heads in agreement. She watched her father clap one of them on the back and then move to another group.

Under all this, the hi-fi was playing softly. Then someone turned it up; then someone put on a disco record; then one young couple started dancing.

The drinks moved in and out of the crowd swiftly; the sweet smell of pot mingled with the cigarette smoke.

A man grabbed Angie's hand and danced her into the small circle that had formed at one end of the living room. Angie did love dancing, and she couldn't help getting caught up in the sensuous rhythm. But the man wasn't really dancing with her. He was dancing with himself and soon drifted off, and she was left foolishly alone. Quickly, she stepped out of the open sliding door onto the slate deck of the pool.

It was cool and almost quiet on the deck. She went over to the darkened canopy and pulled out a chair. "Hi," said a soft, slurred male voice.

She turned to see Don Nagle standing behind her, drink in hand.

"I think you've got the right idea," he said. He pulled another chair out from under the canopy. "Too noisy in there."

Angie didn't know what to say. She didn't want to be trapped by this unpleasant man, but she didn't know how to get out of it.

She smiled uneasily. "Yes," she said, "it is noisy."

He pulled the two chairs together, patted the arm of one. "Come, sit."

She couldn't be rude. The man was Daddy's friend, or at least had been Daddy's client. And he wasn't at all unpleasant to look at. Actually he was quite handsome; women admired him. Angie should be flattered. Right now, she had heard, he was between wives and dating a very big name in films, and here he was wanting to sit with Angie just to get away from the noise. She really couldn't be rude.

He smiled at her. "Do you know why I came to this party?"

She shook her head.

He chuckled. "Just to be with you."

Angie laughed, but not convincingly. Nagle had enough money to make outrageous statements without being called on them. He could say what he wanted and always did. You couldn't put him down unless you had more money than he did, and there weren't many in that position. Why didn't Daddy hate him?

"Angie?"

"Yes, sir."

He laughed loudly. "Yes, *sir*?"

"I mean, yes, Mr. Nagle."

He took a gulp of his drink, set the glass on the deck. "Yes, Don," he said.

"Yes, Don."

He leaned toward her, put his hand over hers. "I came here to see you." He looked in at the dancing crowd in the living room. "Oh, I know your old man is going to put the bite on me before the evening is over, but I don't mind." He pressed her hand a little harder. "We'll hide here. Nobody'll miss us. Okay?"

Angie began to feel a touch of panic.

He leaned forward, looked into her face. "You're a very beautiful girl, Angie."

"Thank you," Angie said, barely audible.

He smiled, leaned back in his chair. "I'd like to go to bed with you."

She was shocked, startled.

He laughed. "Anything wrong with that?"

She couldn't answer.

"Of course not," he answered himself. "Perfectly natural."

She wanted to jump up and run but he was holding her hand firmly.

"What's natural is good. Am I right?"

Now he leaned forward again. He put his other hand on the back of her neck under her hair and began rubbing her neck gently.

She couldn't stand it. She jumped up.

But, anticipating the move, he was just as quick. He put his arms around her and tried to kiss her.

"Let me go, please," she pleaded, turning her head to avoid the kiss. That made him more demanding. He held her tightly, pressing his body into hers.

Suddenly they were wrenched apart. Jim took one wild swing that caught Nagle on the back of the head and sent him skidding into the chair and down on the deck.

"Go inside, Angie." Jim said.

But Angie stood there, hand over her mouth.

Nagle got to his feet. Jim faced him, pumping his fists, really meaning it.

"All right, all right," Nagle said with a mocking smile. "I'll go peacefully."

"You'll go fast!" Jim said tensely. "And if you ever come near her again . . ."

"Okay, I get the message," Nagle said. "But look, nothing happened, it was just . . ."

"Get out!"

"Come on, Jim, playing outraged papa doesn't look good on you."

Now Jim piled into him. They swung wildly, knocking over the chairs, ending up in a wrestling hold, unable to hit each other.

"Okay," Nagle puffed. "I'm going."

Jim shoved him off.

Backing off, Nagle said, "Want to talk a little business, Jim?"

Jim picked up a chair menacingly, and Nagle knew it was time to go. He hurried into the living room, dissolved into the crowd.

Jim led Angie slowly back into the house. He stopped inside the door and held a handkerchief to his cut lip.

"Are you all right, Daddy?" Angie asked anxiously.

He nodded.

Fran saw him standing at the door and hurried over. "What happened?" she asked worriedly.

"Nothing."

He looked at the now wildly gyrating dancers. "Is there any way to get them to all go home, Fran? I'm afraid the party's about over."

He took Angie down the hall to her room, walking slowly. Angie knew he had blown it, pitched his last chance out the window with Nagle and the others. Why hadn't she stayed in the house or run back in the moment she saw Nagle?

They went into her room and Daddy closed the door behind them.

"I'm sorry," Angie said.

He took her in his arms and patted her shoulder gently. "I'm the one who ought to be sorry, getting you into a thing like that. I know about him. I shouldn't have let him in the house."

"It's all right," Angie mumbled.

"No, it isn't all right. I almost got you into my little con game." He tilted her head up to look at him. "No more, Angie. We take our lumps from here in. No more games, okay?"

Angie nodded.

A drop of blood from Jim's lip landed on the elegantly tapered sleeve of the green dress. But it didn't matter. She wouldn't ever wear it again.

Chapter Twelve

"You've got to get out of this house. For a day, anyway," Gloria said firmly.

"I know," Angie answered. "But I get this feeling that something awful will happen if I leave."

"What more awful could happen?"

Angie looked down into her coffee, not answering.

"Come on," Gloria said. "You need a look at the ocean."

Angie shook her head. "You go. Take Edie."

"Never mind Edie."

"I can't go, Gloria." She gestured helplessly around the kitchen. "It'll all fall apart."

Gloria sighed. "Is your mom back?"

Angie nodded.

"How bad is it?"

"Bad. She moved out of their bedroom."

"That bad, huh?"

"Worse. They talk; they hold hands; they moon around the house; and she says she doesn't want any community property. And he laughs and says it's a good thing because they haven't got any. And then they get awfully serious and talk about custody of us."

"Grisly," Gloria said.

"Like we were valuable furniture or something." She sighed. "What's the matter with them?"

"Why don't they act like grown-ups?"

"No, that's the trouble; they do act like grown-ups."

"Can't you sit both of them down . . ."

Angie shook her head. "I tried when Mom came back, and we had hamburgers out at the barbecue. But she just froze up and went back to her room. I love them, but they're awfully mixed up."

"Yeah," Gloria sympathized.

"And they talked about joint custody," Angie said morosely. "As if they're going to slice us up, one hunk for each."

Gloria touched Angie's hand gently.

"That is," Angie went on, "if Daddy doesn't go to jail."

"Aw, Angie . . ."

"He could, Gloria." She looked up at her friend. "I can't believe it. I can't see it happening; I can't see what's after that . . . after they take him away." She took a deep breath. "But it could happen. What'll I do then?"

"It'll work out," Gloria soothed.

"I'd miss him so."

"Angie . . . let's go to the beach."

Angie sighed. "Okay." But she didn't move. She stared down into her coffee cup.

Gloria waited. "Angie . . ." she said softly.

"No, I can't. I really can't. Anyway, I think Ryan's coming over."

"Oh. Well, why didn't you say so?"

"I'd rather go to the beach."

Gloria was surprised. "You'd rather . . ."

"He sounded awful over the phone."

"Ryan?"

Angie nodded.

"Your Ryan?"

"Just awful. He said, 'I want to talk to you,' in this

ridiculous stuffed-shirt voice. Like he was his mother or something.''

"Your Ryan?" Gloria repeated.

Angie stood up abruptly, upsetting the coffee cup. "Let's go to the beach, anyway. I don't care if Ryan comes over! I don't care if the whole house falls down!''

Angie put on her swimsuit. It was a new one-piece that daringly covered most of her body. She slipped her jeans and a loose shirt over the suit.

Gloria had the top down on the Rabbit. As they left the driveway, Angie looked back with the feeling that the house might not be there when they returned.

Gloria turned onto Sunset Boulevard, headed west. It was a warm, sunny day. A day for the beach, and Angie, looking fondly at Gloria, thought of the other days at the beach, of the times they went to Edie's place in Venice, of the day of the roller skates. That was a day!

It was Angie's first time on Venice Beach, and a wild culture shock. Edie's apartment was only half a block from the ocean. They came out of the apartment with their skates on and rolled down to the narrow cement walkway that snaked along the edge of the beach.

It was another world, a fantasy life-style halfway between squalid poverty and Disneyland. A shifting, motley crowd, dressed with rebellious individuality, moved along the cement walk as if drawn to some mysterious carnival in the distance.

Angie, Gloria, and Edie joined the skaters, the cyclists, the joggers, the old ladies carrying paper bags of health food, the shadowboxers punching their imaginary way to title fights in a hazy future.

Sights, sounds, smells. The old hotel, where elderly men sat playing card games at outside tables; the primitive murals on the walls of crumbling warehouses; the sound of transistors blaring out rock tunes, smothering the earnest guitarist sitting crosslegged on the sand and singing a sad song of vanished love. And the smell of barbecued bits of indeterminate meat scraps, of empty beer bottles, of popcorn machines.

They skated down the cement strip, with Angie caught up in the ragged splendor of it all. As they rounded a turn in the walk, a lone skater, squarely in the middle, came toward them.

He was tall, muscular, his skin burned by the sun to a polished walnut. He wore a set of earphones over long, dark hair that framed a scowling, almost handsome face. He was wearing blue shorts and a bright red tank top with white letters that spelled out "No Nukes."

They had to split up to let him through. Obviously he was absorbed in his music and couldn't be bothered with anything in his way.

Edie smiled as he went through and said, "Hi, Jackson." He didn't change his scowl of concentration as he went by, but he definitely noticed Angie. Not the golden Gloria, but Angie. He noticed her.

He spun around a few yards behind them and skated back. Edie gave him space to join them.

"There's no use introducing him," Edie said. "He never takes off those earphones."

Jackson paid no attention to Edie. He just looked down with a half-smile at Angie.

"Who is he?" Gloria asked.

Edie shrugged. "A type. You see lots of types down here. If he's inclined, he skates with you."

"Doesn't he ever talk?"

"If he feels like it."

"What does he do?" Angie asked.

Edie smiled. "He leads movements. No nukes, no oil, rent control, environment. He's against City Hall. When he does talk he can tie a crowd in knots."

Jackson kept looking at Angie. Then, without any self-consciousness, as if it were perfectly natural, he put his arm around her waist.

"Hey!" Angie said.

"It's okay," Edie laughed.

"It's not okay. I don't know this guy."

"He doesn't care. He likes the way you skate."

And, indeed, it seemed as if he did. He matched his stride to hers, and the hand around her waist wasn't amorous or lusty; it was the hand of a partner leading the dance.

"Tell him to let go," Angie said, not too forcefully.

Jackson smiled down at her, brought her back to the rhythm with a gentle pressure.

Gloria was amused. "I think he's cute."

"Yeah," Angie said nervously.

Edie laughed. "Enjoy it. This isn't Oakmont."

It certainly wasn't. Here she was, skating with a total stranger's arm around her waist, rolling down Venice Beach like any one of the outrageous natives.

Now Jackson took her left arm and gently put it around his waist. They were joined in harmonious rhythm, their skates moving smoothly together.

She looked up at Jackson. He was smiling, whether at her or his music she couldn't tell. Then he nodded his head, looking forward. Without words, she knew what he meant. They skated ahead strongly, leaving Edie and Gloria behind.

Before them, the walk was clear. They moved as one person, picking up the tempo slightly as if in a dance, with the music urging them on. Perhaps the music in Jackson's headphones was doing just that.

Angie gave herself to the magic of the moment, to the sound of the breaking surf as they neared the water, to the feel of the fresh salt wind that came off the top of the waves.

Then she felt a stab of awful guilt. Here she was, her arm about a total stranger, feeling a wonderful forbidden closeness. What would Ryan think? What would anyone think? She hadn't even said hello to this guy. It was incredible, disgraceful.

The stab of guilt had thrown her off rhythm. Jackson could feel it. He disengaged his arm, made a graceful turn, and skated back toward Edie and Gloria.

Angie felt inexplicably bereft, abandoned. And even guiltier. She wanted him to come back and skate with her again. It was ridiculous. Should she tell Ryan? Tell him what? Well, there was this stranger and I had this dreadful feeling that I wanted him to keep on holding me forever. Does that make sense, Ryan? No, Angie, it doesn't.

Slowly, she skated back to catch up with them. They had stopped outside a snack bar and were looking at her, waiting. She rolled up to them.

"Jackson's hungry," Edie said.

Angie didn't want to meet Jackson's eyes. She felt he would see through her, sense how much she was attracted to him. Another stab of guilt.

Now, finally, Jackson took off his earphones. They could hear the music. "Mozart," Jackson said. "Number thirty-nine, second movement, andante." He switched off the earphones, turned to Edie. "You got any change?"

"We can manage," Edie said.

Jackson took Angie's arm and skated her to one of the outside tables. The other girls followed.

They sat down, and Jackson looked at the menu on a billboard over the service counter. "You want a burger and fries?" he asked Angie.

She wasn't crazy about burgers and fries, but she said quickly, "Sure, that's fine."

The waiter came over. Jackson looked at Edie and Gloria. They nodded. "Four burgers and fries," he ordered.

When the waiter had gone, he turned to Edie. "You sure you can hack this?"

"It's on me," Gloria said lightly. "I got paid today."

He seemed to notice Gloria for the first time. He smiled at her. "I'll bet you never worked a day in your life."

Gloria returned the smile. "No, I never did."

Jackson turned to Edie. "Couple of rich kids, huh?"

"From Bel-Air," Edie said, with just the slightest touch of malice.

"What do you call them?"

Edie laughed. "This one's Angie; this is Gloria."

"I'm Jackson," he said. "I've never been to Bel-Air. I haven't got a car."

"He's deprived," Edie said.

"Yeah, I'm deprived." He smiled. He touched his hand to Angie's shoulder. "I like this one."

Angie didn't know what to say. His hand on her shoulder was friendly and at the same time caressing. Or was that her imagination? All she could do was smile foolishly.

"She skates real nice," Jackson said.

"So we noticed," said Edie.

He looked directly at Angie. "Do you think I'm attractive, Angie?"

Angie wanted to shout, yes, yes, I do, but what she said was, "Could I have coffee with my fries?"

Jackson laughed, signaled to the waiter who was at the counter watching the burgers. "Four coffees!" He put his headset on the table, turned the switch on. A surprising volume of music came out of the two small earphones.

Listening closely, he ignored the girls. "Hey, this is nice. Listen." He bent close to the earphones. "Cesar Franck, *Fugue and Variations*."

"Couldn't we do a little better than that?" Edie asked.

He frowned. "Shut up and listen."

They listened till the waiter brought the burgers, then Jackson switched off the music. He wolfed down his burger before any of the girls had even removed or added onions to theirs.

He smiled. "Picky eaters, huh?"

Gloria dropped several slices of onion onto her jeans and Jackson picked them off and ate them. He stuffed a handful of fries in his mouth, chewed vigorously, sloshed it all down with coffee.

"Okay," he said. "Angie and I are going skating." He stood up and made a beckoning gesture to Angie.

"Hey, wait," Edie said, "we're going to a movie."

"She's seen that movie," Jackson said. Then to Angie: "You've seen that movie, right, Angie?"

"I guess I have." Angie got to her feet.

Edie frowned. "I don't know if I trust you, Jackson."

He laughed. "You coming, Angie?"

Angie didn't look at Edie, fearing Edie might be shaking her head.

"I won't be long," Angie said vaguely.

Edie shrugged. "Okay, be back for dinner, or we send out the bloodhounds."

Jackson took Angie's arm lightly and they skated out to the cement strip. He slipped the headset under his belt and switched it on. The music had changed now, and a voice was telling them that this was listener request time, and that Miss Maria Martinez of Inglewood had asked for the piano music of Debussy.

Without words, they put arms around each other's waists. The delicate, dancing notes of an arabesque drifted up from the earphones.

Angie was not conscious of skating, but rather she felt lightly airborne a few feet above the path. There was no need to say anything. The pressure of his hand, the touch of his shoulder was enough.

They went up and down the length of the walk many times over. The sun began to retreat, making long, swaying shadows in front of them.

At the end of the last run, the cement walk was deserted. They stopped. Jackson led her onto the sand. They took their skates off and walked barefoot down to a rising dune near the water.

They sat on the sand, looking out. Jackson put his arm around her. She turned to him, and they kissed.

And it was as if they had known each other forever, and this was a parting kiss, the end of something that had been wonderful. They both felt it and clung to each other a very long time. And then a large wave rolled up and swirled around their bare feet.

Jackson sat up, touched her lips with his once more. "Okay," he said, "time to go home now."

Yes, that had been a day! Angie shook her head, coming out of the memory. The Rabbit was now hurrying along toward the beach. She glanced at Gloria, wondering if Gloria would remember the day they had met Jackson. Probably not.

She sighed. Now they were passing the elegant houses that lined both sides of the street, and other memories flooded in on Angie. She thought back to the days the family would all go house hunting, just for fun, and that one wild day when Daddy brought them to Bel-Air, pretending he was just looking, and then bought the house.

What if he hadn't? What if they'd stayed in the Valley? But she knew now that they couldn't have stayed; that the upward pressure, the push for success, for money, position, status, was built into their middle-class dream. She didn't put it into those words, but she felt it.

And she wasn't totally blameless. She had loved going to Oakmont, loved the trip to Europe and having a horse of her own at school. She hadn't rejected the life-style.

Gloria parked the car near Lifeguard Station Eighteen, where all the young people gathered. There were still a few days left of vacation, and the beach was full of color, action, and music.

They looked at the crowd around Station Eighteen. "Feel better?" Gloria asked.

"I think I might survive."

"Good girl. Let's go."

But Angie was lying. She didn't belong out there with all the fun and games; she didn't belong back where they had come from either.

They walked through the hot sand, dodging the volley-ball games and the errant Frisbees. They plopped on the sand and Gloria lay back luxuriously.

"Now," Gloria said, "let's begin living."

Angie smiled, lay back, and looked up at the sky. Why had Ryan been so awful over the phone? What was the matter?

Angie didn't know. He hadn't called in two days, the longest they had ever been out of touch. It couldn't have been just because she went to the beach with Gloria. It had to be something bad, something deep down. Maybe she should call him.

Just a few weeks ago she wouldn't have given it a second thought. She would have picked up the phone and said, "Hey, Ryan, you're neglecting me." And he would have laughed and said he left a note in her mailbox explaining everything and didn't she get the note? And then he would have come over and told her what was wrong, and it would have turned out to be nothing, and he would have taken her in his arms. . . .

"Angie?"

She sighed. "Okay, Mom," she called out.

Angie had been helping with the housework, now that they didn't have Norma. She went down the hall toward the sound of the vacuum cleaner in the master bedroom.

Kathy nodded at one of the beds that was unmade. Jim's bed. Strangely, she let Angie make this bed every morning. The day that Angie went to the beach, the bed wasn't touched.

Angie worked quickly over the noise of the vacuum.

She finished the bed and picked up a dust cloth. Pushing the vacuum into corners and hitting the legs of the bed, Kathy seemed to be angry at the whole room.

But everybody in the house was edgy. It was Friday. They were not edgy because it was Friday but because it was three days from Monday. And Monday, at 10 A.M. sharp, Jim would go into court.

Angie could picture it as if it were on TV. Daddy getting out of the lawyer's car and the two of them going up the courthouse steps and the reporters firing questions and the TV people poking microphones into Daddy's face.

The sound of the vacuum had stopped. Kathy was reeling in the cord. Angie watched her mother pushing the cord into the vacuum handle.

"Mom . . . are you going?"

Kathy looked puzzled. "Going where?"

"To court with Daddy."

Kathy straightened up, frowning. "Angie, we've been over that."

"Mom, the lawyer said it would look better. . . ."

"We've been making things look better for too long, Angie."

"Mom, he needs you!"

"He doesn't need anybody! He never needed anybody! He always went his own way!"

Angie looked at her mother, tried to see past the words. "Mom, you know that's not true!"

Kathy sat on the bed—her bed—with a tired sigh. "No, it's not true. He needs me. But I can't go, Angie. I need me more. I need to be myself. I can't play his games anymore."

Angie could see her grandfather, Kathy's father, standing there saying it.

"I'm going to court, Mom."

"That's up to you."

"I want you to come with me."

"No."

"He loves you."

"That doesn't matter."

"Mom, what does matter?"

"Truth, honesty, discipline! They matter! Sure, it sounds old-fashioned. But to me, these things still matter!"

Angie stared at her.

Kathy started to speak, stopped, got up from the bed. "You finish in here, Angie. I'll start in the living room."

Angie stood in the doorway. "You think he's guilty."

Kathy faced her daughter. She drew a deep breath. "Yes," she said softly.

Angie turned away from the doorway. Kathy reached out, took her in her arms, pressed her close. But Angie stood rigid as rock. Kathy dropped her arms.

"Can't you see how I feel, honey?" Kathy asked.

"You're ashamed of him," Angie said accusingly.

"Angie . . ."

Angie stepped back from her mother. "You're selfish! You're so holy and righteous and awful! He worked for you, for us! He wanted us to have everything! He didn't steal anything; he took a chance! For us! Lots of people take chances. . . ."

"Angie, stop it! Stop playing his game!"

They stood there facing each other, hearts pounding, faces flushed.

Angie lowered her voice. "Please, Mom?"

Kathy shook her head.

Angie turned and ran down to her bedroom. The slam of her door would have shaken the house, except that this was a Bel-Air house built of the very best materials.

She looked at the calendar in despair. This was the last day of Ryan's vacation. He hadn't called; he hadn't left that love-restoring note in the mailbox.

She threw the tennis ball absently, and Duke rushed after it. He bounced against the net and got one hind leg tangled. He pulled the net angrily. But it didn't matter about the net. Whoever bought the house could certainly afford a new net.

Angie sat on the spectator bench and picked up another ball. It wouldn't matter about losing the house either. They'd find something else.

They? Which they? Mom and she? She and Daddy? Nick was out of it. Joint custody? Could a person in jail have joint custody?

Duke dropped the ball at her feet. As she looked up to throw it, she saw Ryan coming through the back gate. As he came toward her, she had a moment of shock, a tick of memory. Something in the way he walked took her back to that first day he appeared at the court. The kid in tennis shorts, carrying a racquet and a can of balls.

She remembered that disarming grin, that insufferable charm as he held out his hand and said, "My name is Ryan; I'm the rich kid who lives at the end of the road."

She wanted to run to him, throw herself in his arms, but she waited. She saw he wasn't smiling.

He opened the gate to the court. "Hi," he said. "I phoned but nobody answered."

"I was out here."

"Yeah, nobody answered."

"When did you call?"

"A little while ago."

Why didn't he hold her, kiss her? Why didn't he tell her everything was all right?

"I was out here with Duke," Angie said.

Hearing his name, Duke wagged his tail and danced in front of the ball. Ryan picked it up and threw it to the far end of the court. They watched Duke chase the ball.

"He's getting old," Ryan said.

"Yeah, I know."

Finally, he said, "You want to talk?"

"Sure. You want a Coke or something?"

"Okay."

They left the court and crossed to the cooler under the canopy. They didn't walk close, touching the way they always did. Angie set two bottles of Coke on the wrought iron table. Ryan took a long time pulling off the caps.

He took a swallow of Coke and then said abruptly, "Your father invited my folks to that party you had the other night."

"What?"

"Your dad. He invited my folks."

"To the party? Our party?"

"Yeah, your party."

"He invited your folks?"

"That's what I just said."

Angie looked puzzled. "When?"

"When what?"

"He didn't tell me. When did he invite them?"

"What difference does it make? He invited them, that's all."

Angie didn't get it. "Well, what's so terrible about that?"

Ryan looked exasperated. "Nothing's so terrible, but don't you see how it looked to my mother?"

"No, I don't see. It just looked like he was trying to be friendly, didn't it?"

"Friendly? After you and I have known each other for all this time? All of a sudden he wants to be friendly with my folks?"

"Why not?"

"Angie, you know why not."

"No, I don't!" she said angrily. "What's wrong with my father inviting . . ."

"What's wrong? It's so obvious!"

"What's obvious?"

"The way it looked to my mother!" he shouted.

"Ryan, your mother has a weird way of looking at a lot of things!"

He glared at her over his Coke. "Okay, I'll spell it out! Your father's in a financial spot! It wouldn't look so bad to his friends if my folks were there."

"Because your folks are stinking rich! Your folks have class!"

"You got it!"

"And maybe my father could use your father's position . . ."

"You've got it again! That's what my mother thought!"

"I don't like your mother, Ryan."

He shrugged. "She's not easy."

"Why didn't you just tell her she was thinking in the wrong direction?"

"Was she?"

"Ryan!"

He turned his face away from her anger. "Okay, okay, she only knows what she reads in the paper. Your father's trying to raise money . . ."

Angie stood up, threw her Coke in the wastebasket. "I'm sorry he invited your folks! I'm glad they didn't come! I'm glad you didn't come! It was a rotten party anyway!"

Ryan saw that he had pushed too far. "Okay, Angie, let's forget it." He held out his arms. "C'mere."

Angie didn't move.

He grinned. "All right, if I've got to be the aggressor . . ." He stood up.

"What you've got to be, Ryan, is something more than mama's boy."

He was stung. "Now, wait a minute . . ."

"You let her think for you, put her rotten ideas inside your head! You're not you anymore!"

Angie was appalled at her own words. Was she saying this to Ryan? Her Ryan? Her one steadfast star, the one she could count on? Was this half-smiling, slack-jawed stranger her Ryan?

"Angie, I've had enough hassle at home," he said wearily.

Unbelieving, she looked at him.

"Come on, Angie, we're fighting about nothing."

"You'd better go home, Ryan."

"You don't mean that."

"I mean it."

"Okay, but if I go . . ." He left the words hanging.

Angie stared at him, saying nothing.

He turned abruptly and walked toward the back gate. Duke came running and dropped the ball at Ryan's feet. Ryan picked it up. With all the strength of his anger, he threw the ball out over the pool and into the ravine below.

Duke ran around the deck and stood puzzled, waiting for the ball to bounce. He turned and ran back to Angie. She bent to one knee and patted him, looking toward the gate that Ryan had closed. In her head, she could see Ryan walk angrily up the road, open the big front door to his house. She could imagine him going in, closing the door.

Duke whined, put a paw on her knee. She patted him, looked toward the gate, for an instant willing Ryan to come back, knowing he wouldn't. She felt stabs of anger, hurt, humiliation. How could he say it? That her father wanted to use his family. A friendly invitation to a party. Of course it was. It had to be. What else?

Angie, come off it. Face it. Be honest. Daddy invited them deliberately. Daddy is desperate for money. That's why he threw the party. Ryan's folks have money. The drowning man grasping at the straw, wasn't that it?

She heard her father's car coming in the driveway. She couldn't talk to him now. She ran quickly to her room.

Chapter Thirteen

It was Sunday.

The sky was a leaden, unforgiving gray. Angie sat by the pool, listlessly turning pages of the Sunday paper.

She knew she had to get out of the house before her folks got up, before the unsolved problems filled the rooms with suppressed, electric tensions. She couldn't bear to see them being polite at breakfast, acting out the civilized dance of divorce, saying inconsequential things to hide the pain.

She put the paper together carefully and took it into the breakfast room, setting it in front of Daddy's chair.

Daddy. She had avoided him since Ryan had told her about the invitation to the party. She couldn't face him. She was angry. It all looked now as if her father would stop at nothing to gain his ends. It seemed as if he had used them all: his wife, his friends. It almost seemed as if he'd used her, Angie. Hadn't he spoiled it all between Mom and himself? Hadn't he spoiled it all between Angie and Ryan?

Somehow, she felt Daddy had betrayed her. And yet, at the same time, deep in her gut, she was sorry for him. He'd spoiled it all for himself most of all.

Confused, she tried to sort out her feelings. But it was impossible. It was as if the father she had known, loved, and admired all her life was suddenly gone. And she was left alone, grieving. Grieving for someone that hadn't been real but was only an image she had built up in her own mind.

She heard him running the shower in his bathroom. He'd be coming in to breakfast in a few minutes. She didn't know what she was going to say. She didn't know anything anymore.

Her insides churning, she felt splintered in all directions, as if she were ready to explode. She had to get out, get away, run.

Where would she go? It didn't matter, really. Just to get away, that was enough. Without conscious direction she went out the breakfast room door and walked to the garage. She looked up at the sky. It could rain.

So it rains; just get out. Take the bike and go. Yes, that was it, the bike. Go on the back streets to nowhere, anywhere, just as long as it wasn't the house.

The bike felt good, alive; like a young animal eager to go; its downturned handlebars were alert to Angie's guiding hands.

She took the hill easily, the strong pumping effort turning away thought; the only goal at the moment was the top of the hill.

She didn't plan any of it, but working against the hills seemed the way to go, as if at the top of any one there might be some mystic, revealing view, some kind of message. And being on top of the hill always brought the unspoken feeling of command, of being in charge of things.

There was a need for this feeling; she needed once again to be in charge of her own life that had so quickly gotten out of hand.

There were no cars on the early morning roads. Angie read the street signs, but the names had no significance. *Linda Flora, Sorrento, Bienvenida.* She had never biked up the "mountains." They weren't really mountains, just long hills separating Bel-Air from the Valley, hills with houses clinging to their steep sides. Cliff-hangers, the houses were called.

A big black dog came rushing off a lawn, growling ferociously, baring his teeth, snapping at the pedals. Angie yelled at him. "Go home! Get away!" He followed her with sullen menace, then, beyond his territory, stopped and walked back stiff-legged, turning his head to be sure she had gone.

Angie's heart was pumping wildly. Around a curve in the road she stopped and leaned her head down, gripping the handlebars. Suddenly she felt terribly alone, unprotected. No one in the streets, no life anywhere, the gray sky oppressive. She was abandoned, lost.

If only Ryan were beside her on his bike.

She looked up, almost expecting to see him, but the deep, knotting pain in her stomach told her that she wouldn't ever see him. That too, lost, gone forever.

She lifted her head. Maybe she ought to turn back. No, not yet. One more hill; keep going up.

Unaware of north, south, east, or west, she took any street upward. Then, all at once, she was on top, on the road that ridged the mountain. And there below was the Valley.

She sat on the bike, looking. Slowly, a sense of calm took hold, a lift as her eyes took command of the space that stretched across the Valley to the real mountains on the other side.

Down below, a small break in the clouds let a narrow shaft of sunlight into a cluster of pale yellow buildings. She could hardly believe it, but there it was. Her old school. Lockman Junior High. It had to be! It was!

She released the brake handles, and, losing sight of the school, she began to coast down the winding road. But she was now aware, with a subdued excitement, that she was going back to her old neighborhood. No need to pedal down the hill; just let herself float. It was almost as if she were drifting on an unseen wave that was taking her back home to the Valley.

Then she was there. The first cross street at the bottom of the hill. Lockman Avenue. She coasted silently to the front gate of the school, got off the bike, and walked to the chained front gate.

She stood there, looking in at the deserted yard. In her head, she could hear the yelling at recess, see her friend Sissy running toward her, waving a chocolate bar. She could hear the shrill whistle calling them back to class.

Irresolute, she clung to the gate a long time. No, she would not go by her old house. That would be too much.

Why too much? It was just a house like all the others on the street. Why not just ride by?

She went down Lockman, turned into Malvern, just as she had always done coming home from school. She passed the candy store, and there was old Mr. Rickoff putting out the Sunday papers on the newsstand. She waved, but he didn't recognize her, didn't wave back.

She slowed, going by the familiar streets. So much of her young life had been played out happily on these streets, places where Mom had said Angie went through her "phases." The Girl Scouts phase, the ballet phase, the horse phase, the discovery of boys, the small rebellions, the secret wine tasting at midnight in the park, the forbidden but rejected cigarette, the day she found Duke. All this passed through her mind as she rode the familiar streets.

Then she turned, inevitably, into Myrtle Lane, *her* street. She stopped to look down the short lane to the circle at the dead end. It was as if she had never left. Not a leaf, a tree, or a front yard had changed. There was the Elisons' camper in the driveway, just as it always had been. There was someone shooting baskets in front of the Mendozas'. And there, almost at the end of the lane, she could see the bursting red bulge of bougainvillea at her own house.

She took a deep breath, letting the warm, comforting familiarity of the place take hold of her. She got off the bike, pushed it slowly along the sidewalk.

Hidden by the far side of the body, someone was washing a car in the Petersons' driveway. The washer, a girl about Angie's age, straightened up, sudsy sponge in hand. She squinted at Angie. "Well, hi," she said in a cool, casual voice.

It was Ruthie Peterson. "Hi, Ruthie!" Angie called enthusiastically.

Ruthie came out from behind the car, eyeing the bike dubiously. "Well, what are you doing here? I thought you lived in Bel-Air."

"I do," Angie said. "I'm just taking a bike ride. How's everybody? How's Linda?"

"Who?"

"Linda Evans, from school."

"I don't go to that school anymore."

Linda had been Ruthie's inseparable friend.

"Oh. Where do you go?"

"Jefferson. How come you biked from Bel-Air?"

Angie laughed nervously. "Exercise. How's your mom, Ruthie?"

"Complaining. What else?" Ruthie nodded at the bike again. "Haven't you got a car?"

"Not yet."

"Everybody's been saying you've probably got your own Rolls by now."

Angie tried to laugh again. "No way," she said.

Ruthie pointed to the washed car. "That's mine. They gave it to me when they bought the pickup."

"It's terrific," Angie said.

"It's just a crummy old Plymouth, but it runs."

"You're lucky."

"Yeah." Ruthie looked up at the sky. "Hey, look, I got

to finish this before it rains or something." She squeezed out the sponge. "Nice seeing you, Angie."

"Yeah," Angie said. "Take care, Ruthie."

Ruthie picked up the hose and began spraying the suds off the car.

Angie wanted to turn back now, but she was obviously pointed toward the lane, and it would look peculiar if she turned around.

She pushed the bike slowly past the familiar houses. And there was Sissy's house. She felt a desperate urge to drop the bike and run up Sissy's walk and burst through the door, yelling Sissy's name just like she used to and hearing Sissy's squeal of delight and grabbing Sissy and babbling a thousand questions and sitting down with the family for coffee and the Danish they always had on Sunday mornings.

But it wouldn't work. She knew it.

She was someone else now. Not by choice. Not changed in her affection for Sissy, but inescapably an outsider, no longer of Myrtle Lane, a different species, a world and a mountain apart.

She pushed the bike past Sissy's house. And then she stood in front of number 18 Myrtle Lane. Her house.

She just stood there and looked and kept looking.

An elderly man came out the door. Framed under the bougainvillea, he said in a not too welcoming voice, "Hello, can I help you?"

Angie was startled. "No. I–I was just stopping. I–I used to know the people who lived here."

"Oh?" the man said suspiciously. "You knew them?"

"Yes."

"Well, they don't live here anymore. They bought a fancy place over in Bel-Air." He gestured to the house. "I guess this wasn't good enough for them."

Angie turned her bike around. "Well, thank you," she

said. "I'm sorry I bothered you." She put her foot on the pedal and swung her leg over the bike.

"I hear he got into some kind of trouble with the law," the man said. Then he turned and went back into the house.

Angie pedaled down the lane as fast as she could. Not looking at anything, she raced the bike down the street as if she were being chased. She shot recklessly out into the street, heedless of the screech of brakes, and the angry horn, and the near-miss. She rode furiously out of sight of Myrtle Lane. And then the first big raindrop splatted against her forehead.

She sped on, not caring about the rain, just feeling a desperate need to flee. Pumping furiously, she turned sharply into Lockman Avenue, and the bike spun out suddenly from under her.

She got up painfully. The knee of one leg of her jeans was torn. She could see the small scrape, with blood beginning to come through.

She hobbled to the bike, put out a hand to stop the front wheel, which was still spinning crazily. Then she righted it and limped to the door of the candy store. It was raining hard now, and Mr. Rickoff was lowering the canvas canopy over the newsstand. She left the bike and went into the store.

Mr. Rickoff followed her in. "Can I help you?" he said.

There was no use saying who she was or asking if he remembered her.

"Thank you. I just want to use the phone."

"You got a dime, it's yours," he said.

She made her way into the phone booth, inserted a coin. She could feel the throbbing in her scraped knee, and her elbows were beginning to hurt.

She heard the ringing on the other end. She blinked hard to keep from crying.

Then someone picked up the phone.

"Mom . . . ?"

"Angie! Where are you?"

"Mom," Angie rasped helplessly. "Mom . . . please
. . . come get me!"

Angie lay in bed a long time after she heard her father's
car go down the driveway. She felt as if she never wanted
to get up, never wanted to face the uncertainty, the plotless,
unstable future that waited just outside the bedroom door.

At least she could have said, "Good luck, Daddy," or
something like that. Good luck? What kind of good luck
could there be? She tried to look ahead, but she couldn't
see anything. No house. No school. No family. No friends.
Nothing.

She got out of bed and dressed slowly. The calendar
on her desk pointed needlessly to the date. The calendar didn't say it, but it might have been printed in
bold letters: MARCH TWENTY-FOURTH, ARRAIGN-
MENT OF JAMES CAREAU, SUPERIOR COURT, TEN
O'CLOCK. She tore the date off the pad, crumpled it,
threw it into the wastebasket.

There was only one thing to do. No, there was only one
thing *not* to do. Just don't think. Blank out. Or fill up your
head with junk. Recite the kings of England, or the preposi-
tions that take the ablative.

"*A, ab, absque . . .*" Then the pain of remembrance, of
Edie drilling her for the Latin test way back that first year
at Oakmont. Well, don't think of Edie; don't think of
Ryan. Don't think!

Fat chance! It was like the ancient formula for making
gold. You put all the right things into the pot and you
stirred. But while you stirred there was one thing you
absolutely must not do. You must not think of the word
"hippopotamus" or the pot wouldn't turn to gold.

She smiled thinly. Thinking happened by itself; you couldn't put it down no matter what. _

She dressed, went into the kitchen, and fed Duke. She poured herself some orange juice and turned on the electric coffee pot.

Duke didn't know it was March twenty-fourth, one jump from the end of the world. He went right on knocking his kibble out of the pan and crunching loudly.

Absently watching Duke, Angie sipped her orange juice. She looked up when she heard her mother's footsteps.

Kathy was dressed in a subdued but very smart gray suit, and her hair looked as if she had just come out of one of those very chic salons in Beverly Hills.

"Hi," Angie said dully. "Where are you going?"

Kathy didn't answer. She tilted the coffee maker and let it fill her cup. Slowly, she brought the cup to the table and sat down. She took a sip of coffee.

"Mom . . ."

Kathy took another sip of coffee, carefully set the cup in the saucer.

"I'm going to court to be with Daddy."

Angie stared at her.

Kathy looked at her watch. "We've got time if you want to get dressed, Angie."

"You're going to court?" Angie said unbelievingly.

"Yes." She looked at Angie tenderly. "I'd like it if you'd come with me."

"You're going to be with him? After all he's done?"

"Angela, I know it's hard to explain . . ."

"Hard to explain!" Angie said angrily. "How can you even think of it!"

"I've been thinking of it for days. I know all the reasons why I shouldn't. I know what he's done. . . ."

"And you're going anyway !"

"Yes."

"Why? Why?"

"I don't know. I just know I have to be there."

"He needs you," Angie said scornfully.

Kathy nodded. "Yes. And he needs you too."

"I needed Ryan! And what happened? In one minute, one stupid, selfish phone call to Ryan's parents, he ruined it!"

Kathy nodded. "I know."

"You know! Then why . . ."

Kathy shrugged helplessly. "I love him. I want to be with him."

"And you're going to divorce him!"

Kathy sighed. "Come with me, Angie."

Angie turned away from her mother's pleading look.

Kathy came over, kissed her on the top of the head, and went out the kitchen to the garage. Angie could hear the car start, back out, and go down the driveway.

She picked up her coffee cup and threw it with all her strength at the kitchen window. With a terrible crash, the window broke; the cup shattered into the sink. She flung her arms on the table and buried her head in the darkness of her sweater.

She might have stayed there an hour, or she might have stayed there for five minutes. Angie raised her head to see the broken window. She wondered idly if anyone would get around to fixing it before the house was sold.

She felt drained, battered, confused. She could picture her mother walking up the courthouse steps, looking just right, smiling just right. And meaning it. Being there with him because he needed her. Okay, because she loved him. Well, I love him too, Angie thought angrily. But does that make him the White Knight or something? Does that wipe the whole slate clean?

She didn't hear Gloria's car come up the driveway, but Duke barked a few beats ahead of the front doorbell.

"It's open!" Angie yelled.

Gloria came in and gave Angie a quick hug. "Hey, why aren't you dressed?" she asked.

Angie shrugged, leaned back in her chair.

"We're going down to be with your dad, right?"

"We?"

"Yeah, I invited myself, okay? I figured your mom's not going, and Nick isn't here, so your dad needs extra troops. Right?"

"Mom went."

"She did?"

"Yeah. She loves him," Angie said flatly.

Gloria laughed. "Terrific. We all love him, and we'll all be there to hold his hand."

"You really mean that, don't you?"

"Of course I do. So he's a lousy business man, and he's in trouble." She paused, looked searchingly at Angie. "So what if he *is* a crook?"

Angie's head snapped up. "Now wait a minute. Who said he's a crook?"

"You did. Lots of times. Or words to that effect."

"I never said he was a crook."

"Okay, a swindler."

Angie stiffened. "I didn't say that, either."

"All right, a thief, a con man, whatever. But that's why you're not going to court with him, isn't it?"

Angie started to answer but Gloria went on: "Guess it would be kind of embarrassing," she said indulgently. "I understand."

Angrily, Angie stood up. "You don't understand anything!"

"Come on, Angie, he broke the law. Everybody knows that. Who could expect you to . . ."

"Hold on a second! He never robbed anyone. He gambled, he never stole. He's not a thief! He mismanaged funds, that's all."

"Sure," Gloria said. "I know."

"What do you know? You don't know how hard he's trying to pay back his clients. And he'll do it, too. He'll make restitution, you'll see!"

Gloria shrugged. "Okay, okay, forget it. Whatever he is, it doesn't matter to me." She gave a short laugh. "Me, I like the guy."

"You're just like all the rest!" Angie yelled. "Nobody called him a crook when he made big money for his clients. They cheered him on. When he tripled their dollars, they took the money and ran. They didn't call him a swindler then! Nobody pinned labels on him then. Nobody questioned him then."

"Neither did you . . . then," Gloria answered softly.

"I never had any reason to question him. I believed in him—I still do. I . . ." She stopped in mid-sentence, stared at Gloria.

The two stood there for a long moment, eyes locked. Angie was surprised, amazed at her own words. *I'm defending him. Standing up for him. I can't understand . . .*

And then it all fell into place in her mind. Okay, he made a mistake, a bad one. But it couldn't change what he meant to her. The love he'd always given her had to count for something. Right or wrong, he was Dad, the same wonderful father as always.

Still looking into Gloria's eyes, she shrugged helplessly. Then, in a small voice, she said, "I love him too."

Gloria smiled. "Why don't you go get dressed, Angie?"

Holding hands, the girls flew across the wide pavement to the courthouse steps. Angie couldn't see her parents but knew they were there, hidden behind the knot of people moving up the stairs. She could hear reporters calling out questions; she could see the flash of cameras. TV mobile units angled down on the crowd.

Angie let go of Gloria's hand and took the steps two at a

time. She pushed her way into the tight group. "Let me through! I'm his daughter! Let me by!"

The crowd gave way and she caught sight of her mother and father, moving with the attorney toward the entrance. "Wait for me! Daddy! Dad, wait!"

Jim turned, looked at her as Angie, panting, reached his side. He looked puzzled, as if he couldn't believe she was really there.

Fighting for breath, Angie looked up into his eyes.

"Angie, I'm glad," she heard her mother say.

She was still gasping for breath when she felt Gloria beside her. Then she was suddenly blinded by lights as flashes went off in her face.

Through the pinpoints of colored circles dancing before her eyes, she saw her dad look over her head at the reporters. "This is my daughter, Angela," he said in a clear, distinct voice. He nodded at Gloria. "And a close friend of the family."

"Let's go," the attorney said as he swung open the doors.

Jim quickly kissed Angie on the cheek. Then he turned, took Kathy's arm and went into the courthouse.

Angie stood there swallowing her tears. Whatever happened now, there was no turning back, no more doubts. That was the only way it could ever be.

A reporter edged closer. "Miss Careau?"

She turned. She somehow knew he would ask if her father was going to plead guilty or not guilty.

She looked up at the reporter. No matter how her father pleaded, or what he had done, it made no difference to her now.

She smiled and lifted her head proudly. "No comment," she said.

About the Authors

ANNE SNYDER, in addition to writing books and educational material, is active in the field of television. She is also a teacher of creative writing, and has taught at Valley College, Pierce College and University of California, Northridge. Her novel, *First Step,* published by Signet in paperback, was a winner of the Friends of American Writers Award, and became an ABC-TV Afternoon Special. *My Name Is Davy— I'm an Alcoholic; Goodbye, Paper Doll; Counter Play; Two Point Zero* and *Nobody's Brother* are also published by Signet. She and her husband live in Woodland Hills, California.

LOUIS PELLETIER, co-author of *The Best That Money Can Buy, Two Point Zero,* as well as *Counter Play,* includes among his many TV credits such shows as *General Electric Theater, Hawaiian Eye* and *The Love Boat.* Long associated with Walt Disney Studios, he scripted such movies as *Big Red, Those Calloways,* and *The Horse in the Gray Flannel Suit.* A resident of Pacific Palisades, Pelletier has taught screenwriting at University of California, Northridge, and U.C., Riverside.